# The Treasures
# of Weatherby

# Also by Zilpha Keatley Snyder

*And Condors Danced*

*Black and Blue Magic*

*Blair's Nightmare*

*Cat Running*

*The Changeling*

*The Egypt Game*

*The Famous Stanley Kidnapping Case*

*Fool's Gold*

*The Ghosts of Rathburn Park*

*Gib and the Gray Ghost*

*Gib Rides Home*

*The Gypsy Game*

*The Headless Cupid*

*Janie's Private Eyes*

*Libby on Wednesday*

*The Magic Nation Thing*

*The Runaways*

*Season of Ponies*

*Song of the Gargoyle*

*Squeak Saves the Day*

*The Trespassers*

*The Truth About Stone Hollow*

*The Unseen*

*The Velvet Room*

*The Witches of Worm*

# The Treasures
# of Weatherby

## Zilpha Keatley Snyder

Author of *The Egypt Game*

Atheneum Books for Young Readers

New York   London   Toronto   Sydney

Atheneum Books for Young Readers
An imprint of Simon & Schuster Children's Publishing Division
1230 Avenue of the Americas
New York, New York 10020

Book design by Debra Sfetsios and Tom Daly
The text for this book is set in Throhand Regular.

Manufactured in the United States of America
First Edition
2 4 6 8 10 9 7 5 3 1

Library of Congress Cataloging-in-Publication Data
Snyder, Zilpha Keatley.
The treasures of Weatherby / Zilpha Keatley Snyder. — 1st ed.
p. cm.
Summary: Determined to be as strong and powerful as the first Harleigh, who built
the rambling Weatherby Hall, twelve-year-old Harleigh Fourth and an equally diminutive new
friend try to foil the plans of a distant relative who is seeking the long-lost Weatherby fortune.
ISBN-13: 978-1-4169-1398-6 (hardcover : alk. paper)
ISBN-10: 1-4169-1398-X (hardcover : alk. paper)
[1. Family life—Fiction. 2. Buried treasure—Fiction. 3. Size—Fiction.
4. Dwellings—Fiction.] I. Title.
PZ7.S68522Tor 2007
[Fic]—dc22 2006010808

To everyone who listens for whispers

# Foreword

As is sometimes pointed out to me, and as I freely acknowledge, there are certain themes that have repeated themselves in several of my books; one of them being the importance of a *big, old, mysterious house* as the setting, and sometimes almost as a character in the story. It's true. I confess. Of my forty-some books I can think of quite a few in which a big, old house plays an important role.

Why? I can't really say, except that in my real unfictionalized life, I've always been fascinated by big, old houses. In fact, I've lived in a couple. However, I've recently decided that enough is enough. I would allow myself just one more big, old house. And that's it!

So here it is. The biggest, oldest, and most mysterious house of all. In fact, the big, old house story to end all big, old house stories. It's a promise.

# The Treasures
# of Weatherby

# Chapter One

On a warm summer morning in the not-so-distant past, a twelve-year-old boy woke up in a large octagonal room at the top of a tower, and for a startled moment wondered where he was. Dazzled by the bright sunshine that slanted in through the surrounding circle of windows, he sat up quickly, blinking his eyes and shaking his head. But then, of course, he remembered. He remembered that he, Harleigh J. Weatherby the Fourth, was in his own bed, in a room that he had only recently claimed as his own private territory.

His choice of the once famous Weatherby Aerie was part of a larger decision to stop letting other people tell him exactly what he was going to do with his life, and how

and where he was going to do it. Having come to that conclusion, he had inspected, and decided against, a number of large impressive bedrooms on the second floor of Weatherby House—grand suites that included dressing rooms and large, hopelessly old-fashioned bathrooms. He'd even explored the mostly abandoned east wing, where some early Weatherbys had once conducted various family businesses. But he'd found the impersonal offices and dark and dismal conference rooms not particularly inviting.

In making his final choice, he'd rejected not only some interesting possibilities but, more importantly, the advice of certain members of the Weatherby family. His great-aunt Adelaide in particular, who had insisted that the tower room, or the Aerie, as it had been called when she was a girl, was too isolated, and the climb would be far too much for Harleigh so soon after his *surgery*.

It was the mention of the surgery that did it, that set his decision in stone, so to speak. Moving to the tower had been only one of several possibilities until then, but when Aunt Adelaide brought up that stupid, useless operation it reminded Harleigh that he had finished letting other people influence his most important decisions. From now on he would decide where he wanted to live, as well as how, and this time nothing any of them could say would make any difference.

All right, he had more or less agreed to allow the doctors to do that "one last" experiment on his heart, but only because they (his father, Aunt Adelaide, and any number of doctors) had promised that this one last surgery really would make him start to grow. But, as usual, it was a lie. All those aches and pains and long, boring hours in bed and now, four months later, he — the last direct descendant of the builder of the famous Weatherby mansion — was still, at the age of twelve, about the size of your average six-year-old.

Still sitting up in bed, Harleigh shrugged, unclenched his teeth, and reminded himself that he didn't care. Not any longer. Not since he'd come to the conclusion that physical size didn't have anything to do with winning or losing, and that someday he, Harleigh the Fourth, was going to be just as strong and powerful as his famous ancestor. Just as powerful as that first Harleigh J. Weatherby, who, more than a hundred years ago, had made a huge amount of money and then decided to settle down in the small town of Riverbend and build a castle.

Which is exactly what he did. He built and built and went on building. And even now, when most of the Weatherbys were either dead or old and unimportant, that first Harleigh's enormous castle was still there. Perhaps a little dilapidated and old-fashioned in some places, but in many ways as grand and impressive as ever.

And someday he, Harleigh the Fourth, would hire crews of carpenters and squads of stonemasons to repair and modernize the house, and hundreds of gardeners to replant its famous gardens. And then, no matter how tall he was, everyone in Weatherby House, along with all the citizens of Riverbend, would have to look up to him.

That would show them! All of them—including his father and the other Weatherbys who had forced him to go on being the heart surgeons' favorite guinea pig, simply because it embarrassed them that a direct-descendant Weatherby could be so small for his age. And as for certain smart-mouthed people who'd been in his class when he'd spent those two terrible years in the Riverbend public schools—he'd show them, too.

Sliding out of bed, Harleigh Four stomped across the floor to the nearest window and, standing on tiptoe, looked down to where Weatherby House stretched out far and away to the east and to the west like an endless range of mountains, punctuated by turrets and towers and decorated here and there by clusters of fancy chimneys. A mansion so large that a newspaper reporter had once described it as being as grand as Buckingham Palace and as endless as the Great Wall of China. And all of it, all of Weatherby House, would someday belong to him, Harleigh J. Weatherby the Fourth.

Turning away from the window, Harleigh squared his shoulders and inspected his new living quarters critically, but with some satisfaction. The huge eight-sided room, with its ornate tile floor and thick stone walls, made an impressive, if rather barren, bedroom. Besides his narrow bed, the only furniture was a row of marble-topped cabinets, where servants had once set out food and drink for gatherings of long-gone Weatherbys and their guests, who had managed the steep climb in order to watch a famous Weatherby sunset.

His inspection completed, Harleigh selected a pair of khaki shorts, his usual summertime costume, from one of the cabinets, and picking up some other articles of clothing from where he'd dropped them the night before, he headed for the landing and the long winding stairs that led down to the third floor.

In spite of Aunt Adelaide's warnings, he'd never had any problem with the stairs. That last operation, the one that certainly hadn't made him start to grow, did seem to have made a difference in his energy level. And as for the isolation Aunt Adelaide worried about—the privacy, that is—he really enjoyed it. The tower was his now, and if no one else at Weatherby House had the strength and stamina to intrude on his private space, so much the better.

After tromping noisily down two circular flights of

clattering iron stairs and stopping briefly at an old-fashioned but more or less functional third-floor bathroom, he ran the full length of the third-floor ballroom, yelling as he went to set off its surging echoes. Still at high speed, he galloped down a grand, and then a grander, flight of marble stairs, whistled as he made his way through the long, narrow dining hall where enormous portraits of long-gone Weatherbys stared down disapprovingly, slowed to a trot through the elaborate butler's pantry, and finally burst out through the swinging doors that led to the huge central kitchen where, nowadays, almost all family meals were not only cooked but also served and eaten.

The usual people were there to notice Harleigh's energetic entrance, and possibly realize how wrong they'd been when they'd suggested that sleeping in a tower could be dangerous to your health. Only three people, actually, because, not being a Weatherby, Matilda the cook didn't count.

Great-Aunt Adelaide was there, of course, accompanied and waited on as always by Cousin Josephine. And, at the other end of the table, Uncle Edgar. Uncle Edgar wasn't exactly Harleigh's uncle, and Josephine was something like a second cousin twice removed, but it was Aunt Adelaide who insisted on such family titles. Insisted, according to Uncle Edgar, because the titles emphasized

the fact that everyone who lived in Weatherby House had to be a Weatherby in one way or another, or she wouldn't have allowed them to be there.

Cousin Josephine was there in the kitchen, because it was her job to get Adelaide the Great up, dressed, and into her wheelchair. And big, bulky Uncle Edgar was there to eat as much of Matilda's cooking as possible.

One of Aunt Adelaide's strict rules was that Matilda cooked only for *direct* descendants, and neither Cousin Josephine nor Uncle Edgar were all that direct. But since Cousin Josephine was Aunt Adelaide's nurse and companion, and Uncle Edgar was Harleigh Four's tutor, they managed to be exceptions to the rule. The only other really direct descendant, Harleigh Four's father, Harleigh the Third, wasn't there — as usual.

Some of the other Weatherby odds and ends, such as Cousin Alden, who was Josephine's husband, and Cousin A. J., who was (or had once been) a law student, sometimes cooked and ate in the enormous kitchen; but they had to cook their own food and try to keep out of Matilda's way. There were, of course, other much smaller kitchens here and there in the more distant ells and wings of the house, where at least a dozen less directly descended Weatherbys had to make do.

But today Harleigh Four's dramatic entrance was

witnessed only by Great-Aunt Adelaide and Josephine, and to some extent by Uncle Edgar, whose attention was mainly focused on a plateful of Matilda's Belgian waffles. They all looked up when Harleigh burst through the swinging door, but except for a grunt from Uncle Edgar, there wasn't much in the way of a greeting. And if anyone noticed that Harleigh Four was not at all out of breath, they didn't bother to mention it.

In fact, no one seemed to be in a talkative mood, and Uncle Edgar had finished his third waffle before Harleigh heard the good news: There would be no lessons that morning, because his tutor "wasn't feeling up to it."

As Uncle Edgar hoisted himself out of his chair and lumbered toward the door, Aunt Adelaide said, "Oh, I *am* sorry, Edgar. I do hope all those waffles weren't too much for your poor overworked digestive system." Aunt Adelaide was smiling, but as usual, her sharp-toothed smile was almost more threatening than her frown. But if Harleigh Four was hoping for an entertaining argument, it didn't happen. Not this time.

Instead, Uncle Edgar only grinned sarcastically and said, "I didn't say I was ill, Aunt Adelaide. What I don't feel up to is shutting myself and the boy up in that dark dungeon on such a beautiful morning."

Harleigh knew what he was referring to, and he agreed,

more or less. While he had always admired the dark, impressive grandeur of the Weatherby House library, he had to admit it was rather dim and gloomy.

Uncle Edgar did a sideways nod in Harleigh's direction. "Scoot, boy," he said. "Get out into the sunshine before I lose this argument and we get sentenced to . . ."

Harleigh didn't wait to hear the rest. A split second later he was scooting across the main courtyard, circling the dry fishpond and the huge shabby gazebo, on his way to escape into the overgrown jungle that had once been the famous Weatherby House Gardens.

He headed first to his most recent discovery, the sad remains of what had been a formal Italian garden, where a circle of weather-stained gods and goddesses ringed a leaf-cluttered depression—all that remained of a large tile-lined pool where a marble dolphin had once spouted a stream of water high into the air.

The Italian garden was a new find because, until a few weeks ago, Harleigh had rarely ventured much beyond the paved courtyard of Weatherby House. But since his strength and energy had begun to improve, he'd been going farther into the garden every day. He'd already made several interesting discoveries, but he'd not yet found the one thing he'd been especially looking for—the Weatherby House Maze.

He'd heard about the maze over and over again from Great-Aunt Adelaide, who loved to talk about the famous—or once famous—Weatherby House Gardens. According to her, the yew tree maze had been patterned after an ancient one in England, and it had been the high point of any visit to Weatherby House. Important people, Aunt Adelaide said, used to come from all over the country just to see if they could find their way through the Weatherby maze—which, according to her, very rarely happened. Not that they were lost, never to be seen again; but they weren't seen again until they were rounded up by Weatherby rescue parties, usually made up of gardeners who knew the way.

Harleigh felt sure that he, however, could easily solve the maze's mystery, and by doing so he would prove that he, as a directly descended Weatherby, could do just about anything he wanted to. But first he had to find out where it was.

Having made his way through the Italian garden, Harleigh maneuvered around a threatening blackberry hedge and had just pushed his way through a thick stand of bamboo, when he emerged into a clearing that held only one tall tree—and suddenly discovered that he was not alone.

# Chapter Two

She was hanging from the bottom limb of the towering black walnut tree when he first saw her. He had reached the end of the bamboo patch and was reaching out to shove away the last frond, when he glanced up just in time to see a small human being lose her hold on a limb and drop to the ground at least ten feet below.

It was a long drop. So long that for a startled moment Harleigh thought she might be dead or seriously injured, but before he reached her he could tell that she wasn't. Not dead, nor even badly hurt, but apparently very frightened. Crouching close to the ground, her eyes wide with fear, she gasped as she stared up at him through tangled strands of straggly hair.

His first impulse was to demand to know who she was, and what she was doing on Weatherby property. Demand, but perhaps not too angrily, because there was a part of him that couldn't help being pleased with her reaction. He couldn't remember scaring anyone before, and he rather liked the sensation. In the end, it was she who spoke first.

In a small, whispery voice she said, "I know who you are. You're Hardly, aren't you?"

At that point any sympathy he might have been feeling for the terrorized trespasser vanished. She must have known him, or at least known who he was, when he was attending Riverbend Elementary, where some wise guy had changed Harleigh into Hardly. As in "hardly there at all." And the name had stuck. He'd let them all know how he hated the nickname, which apparently only made the whole thing more entertaining.

No one had called him Hardly since Adelaide the Great finally, after many arguments and much pleading, accepted his decision to quit school and go back to being tutored at home. But his reaction to the nickname hadn't changed. Not for a minute. He didn't, however, remember a girl in any of his classes who had looked like . . . Still examining the trespasser through slitted eyes, he asked, "Were you in my class at Riverbend?"

"I wasn't in your class," she said. "But I knew who you

were. And I didn't mean to call you Hardly. It just came out that way. It's easier to say than Harleigh."

Well, maybe that explained it. But it didn't explain what she was doing on Weatherby property. "So." Harleigh raised his head, looking down his nose at the girl, who was still crouching at his feet like a frightened animal. It was for him an unusual point of view. "So—what are you doing here?" he demanded in an appropriately stern tone of voice. "And how did you get through our fence?"

Still peering at him through her straggly, mouse-colored hair, she slowly got up, but surprisingly, not very far up. Once up on her bare feet, it became apparent that she was quite small. Not much taller than Harleigh himself, and not nearly as sturdily built. Her long, clingy dress, which might once have been part of an evening gown or fancy costume, revealed how small and thin she was.

As if suddenly noticing that she was being inspected, the girl rubbed her hands together in a dusting motion and then did the same to the front of her dress. It didn't improve her appearance any, but it did seem to give her confidence. She was almost smiling as she turned her attention back to Harleigh and asked, "What did you say about the fence?"

"I asked," Harleigh said firmly, "how you got through our fence."

"Not through," she said. "Over."

That didn't explain anything. Harleigh shrugged impatiently. "All right, over. How did you get *over* our fence?" He couldn't imagine how that could be true. The high, sword-tipped metal poles that formed the Weatherby fence were, as far as Harleigh knew, absolutely unclimbable by anyone. And certainly not climbable by a small, skinny girl.

She nodded slowly, and then, in a questioning tone of voice, she said, "I flew?"

Harleigh stared for a moment in shocked silence before he snorted and said, "You think I'm going to believe that?"

"No, really," she said. "I did." She was definitely smiling now, smiling thoughtfully, her head tipped to one side. "I could show you if you wouldn't . . ." She paused and then went on. "Are you? Are you going to tell on me?"

"Tell who? Who did you think I might tell?"

She made a sweeping gesture. "The people who live in the castle. There are a lot of them, aren't there. Why are there so many of them?"

Harleigh sighed impatiently. It was a question he himself had asked without getting an answer that seemed the least bit sensible. So now he was surprised to find himself explaining the situation, as if she somehow had the right to know.

"It was in the will. In this will that Weatherby the First left when he died. I guess a lot of his close relatives had died, and

he thought there weren't enough people living in the house, so he made the will say that any Weatherby descendant could live there, for free. So a lot of them do. The oldest direct descendant gets to run things, but all the descendants can live there for free, as long as they obey the rules."

The girl nodded. Her deep gray eyes were wide and glowed as if with extreme excitement. "That's so wonderful," she whispered. "Oh, I do wish I was one. So, are they all very rich? Did the first Harleigh leave lots of jewels and golden treasure?"

"Golden treasure?" Harleigh snorted again. He had an effective snort, not loud—only a puff of air accompanied by a sharp humph—but it expressed his feelings well, particularly negative ones. "No, of course not. Most of them are really poor or they wouldn't live there."

"Oh." She seemed shocked, unbelieving. "Why wouldn't they want to live in such a beautiful place?"

Harleigh's smile was sarcastic. "Some of it's beautiful, all right. But not all of it. And there are rules. Lots of them. Only poor people would put up with all the rules. Like they can't have any visitors unless they bring them to meet my great-aunt first and get her okay. The only one who gets to decide things is my great-aunt."

"And she's very rich?"

"No. That's not what I said. She just kind of runs

things." His smile was rueful. "Well, more than kind of, actually. She pretty much controls everything, because she's the oldest direct descendant. And she also has the Fund."

"What's that? What's a fund?"

"Well, it's . . . ," Harleigh started before it again occurred to him to wonder why he was talking so much. Why was he discussing things with this strange girl that he'd never discussed with anyone before? Certainly not with anyone who wasn't a Weatherby. Perhaps it was the way she seemed so enthusiastic, as if everything he said, and the way he said it, was absolutely fascinating.

"Well," he began again, "the first Harleigh left the Fund. That's what Aunt Adelaide calls it. It was money that was supposed to take care of the property, like pay the gardeners and maids and people like that. I guess when he was alive it was enough to pay for lots of servants, but now it's barely enough to pay for two or three. That's why," he swung his arms, indicating what lay all around them, "why everything is such a mess."

"Oh, no," she said. "It's not a mess. It's beautiful just the way it is. That's why I come here. I love to come here."

"And you get inside the grounds by"—Harleigh made his curled lip and raised eyebrow say he didn't believe it for a minute—"by flying?"

She nodded. He was taking her slightly embarrassed

smile to be a kind of admission that she wasn't telling the exact truth, when to his great surprise, she asked, "Do you want to see me do it?"

"To see you fly? Yes. I sure do." He made another lip twist that said he wasn't the kind of person who would easily be made a fool of. "That is something I'd *really* like to see."

"All right," she said. She turned as if to go, but then turned back. "And you won't tell on me? You won't tell anybody?"

"No," he said firmly, and felt sure he meant it, without stopping to ask himself why. "No. I won't tell on you."

She led the way then, through a tangled jungle of tropical vines, and then past a long wall of thick overgrown hedge. The complicated path went on and on with many turns and twists until, suddenly, there right before them, was the fence—its tall wrought-iron bars topped by a threatening fringe of sharply pointed spears.

Harleigh was still staring at the fence when he realized that she was no longer standing beside him. He turned to see her halfway up the trunk of a tall oak tree that towered over the wall. He'd missed seeing how she got up that far— how in the world she'd managed to make it up the smooth bare trunk to where the first limbs branched out. Continuing to climb, as quick and agile as a monkey, she was hidden for a moment in the crotch of the trunk before she

appeared again crawling out on a high limb. As she climbed higher, he lost sight of her now and then as she disappeared behind leafy branches. And then, suddenly, there she was again far overhead as she flew, or seemed to fly, into a tree that grew outside the fence.

But there had been a rope, hadn't there? She had been swinging from a length of rope, or hadn't she? He was still staring up toward the place where she had disappeared, wondering and arguing with himself, when there she was, on the ground again, but now, just outside the fence.

"See," she was saying with her small, narrow face pressed against the iron rods of the fence. "That's how I do it." She turned as if to go.

"Wait," Harleigh said. "I want to talk to you. I want to know . . ."

She turned back once more, but only long enough to wave. "I have to go now," she called back over her shoulder. "I'll be back tomorrow."

# Chapter Three

In spite of its windowless gloom, the Weatherby House's library had always been Harleigh Four's favorite room. Under a high-domed ceiling, its soaring walls supported shelf after shelf of darkly shining wood. Here and there a series of circular stairs led up to narrow balconies, which gave access to even higher rows of shelves. And every shelf was solidly covered by beautifully bound books. So many books and shelves there was barely enough open wall space for the more-than-life-size oil painting of a frowning man sitting, with a book in his lap, on a thronelike chair. The man in the picture was, of course, Harleigh J. Weatherby the First, and in his great-grandson's opinion the library, of all of the grand Weatherby rooms, was undoubtedly the grandest.

He had to admit, however, that it was a bit gloomy. The famous portrait of Harleigh J. Weatherby the First soared up, from only an inch or so above Harleigh Four's head, when he measured himself on the wall below it, to just below one of the second-floor balconies, completely covering the only space where there might have been room for a panel of windows.

"Poor architectural planning," Harleigh Four's father, Harleigh the Third, liked to say about the library. Harleigh the Third, an architect himself, seemed to spend most of his time criticizing, not only Weatherby House, but also famous buildings all over the world. "Planned for the grand effect," was one of his favorite comments, "rather than for any useful purpose."

Harleigh Four didn't entirely disagree. But, at the same time, he did feel that this kind of picky criticism of Weatherby House didn't serve any useful purpose. He liked the enormous library just the way it was. So what if it was dark and gloomy. There were plenty of lamps, after all, and if it sometimes felt lonely it was only because . . . well, because nowadays no one was allowed to use the library except Harleigh Four and Uncle Edgar. And, as Uncle Edgar liked to say, when he could get anyone to listen, it was quite likely that no one had ever used it very much.

The very next day after Harleigh Four discovered the "flying" trespasser, Uncle Edgar once again brought up his favorite criticism. The picky one about how little time the original Weatherby must have spent in his glorious library. As Harleigh came into the room that morning, Uncle Edgar was holding up a book called *The Iliad* and saying, "We have here in this grand room every book you'd expect to find in the library of a well-educated, highly literate person But not a one, except for the ones you and I have been perusing, looks the least bit loved—or even briefly visited. Not a one that seems a little worn or that falls open easily to a favorite page. No, I'm afraid"—Uncle Edgar pointed up at the painting of Harleigh the First—"our famous ancestor was a bit of a fake in more ways than one. All this"—he waved his big arms and then pointed to the portrait—"that book in his lap, and all these beautiful volumes just to make people think he was a well-read man."

Harleigh tried to copy the frown on the face in the portrait. He didn't see the point in putting down his famous ancestor for unimportant faults, as if he'd only been an ordinary, unimportant person. In the past he'd tried to say so, but today was no time for an argument, or for one of the long rambling discussions that Uncle Edgar liked to get into.

Today Harleigh Four was determined to get away as quickly as possible to see if the mysterious trespasser had

been lying when she said she would be back. So today's lessons needed to be dispensed with quickly, and that was what he set himself to do. By concentrating fiercely on everything Uncle Edgar gave him to read, and on every problem put before him, Harleigh finished all his assignments in record time, surprising not only Uncle Edgar but himself as well.

"My word!" Uncle Edgar exclaimed as he went over the page full of geometry problems Harleigh slapped down in front of him. "I am impressed. And a bit puzzled, too, I must say. To what should I attribute the sudden improvement in our attention span?" His smile widened. "Turning over a new leaf, are we?"

Harleigh didn't return the smile. Instead, he just shrugged impatiently and asked if he could go. Uncle Edgar's broad grin faded into the folds of his fat face. "All right, all right, be off with you," he grumbled, and a few seconds later Harleigh Four was on his way.

Heading for the nearest exit, he crossed the broad entryway at a run and dashed down the wide west corridor as far as the door that led into the glass-roofed greenhouse, or as Aunt Adelaide called it, the solarium. He continued at a run down one of the solarium's narrow aisles, dodging around hanging vines and under huge fronds of exotic plants. Passing old Ralph, the gardener, without stopping to say hello, he

burst out into the open courtyard, where he stopped long enough to catch his breath and decide on his next move.

The next problem was that he wasn't sure if he could remember exactly how he'd arrived at the place where he'd first seen the trespasser. He knew he'd been a long way out into the most neglected part of the property, in an area he'd only started to explore since he'd gotten some of his strength and endurance back. He thought he might have seen that old tree that stood in the midst of a surrounding clearing on one of his recent explorations, but he wasn't sure. It wasn't until he had made several false starts that he stumbled on the bamboo thicket and knew he was on the right track.

But one crooked, narrow path through the bamboo ended only in a thorny blackberry thicket. Back at the beginning of the bamboo, Harleigh chose another heading, which for a time seemed to be slanting in the wrong direction before it ended exactly where he wanted it to—under the same tree the trespasser had been hanging from when he first saw her.

Just as he remembered, several thick limbs branched out from the wide trunk, quite a way off the ground. But today no one was hanging from any of them. And what's more, there seemed to be no way to get up to them. He walked slowly around the thick trunk—the tall, smooth trunk that offered nothing at all that could be used as a hand- or toehold.

Giving up on the trunk, he had gone back to staring up at the limb the girl had been hanging from, when he noticed that this particular limb branched out from where the main trunk divided into three parts, forming a large crotch. And right there in the crotch was something that looked like the edge of a platform, and above it a glimpse of a smooth wooden panel that might be a part of a wall. It really looked as if something had been built high up there in the tree.

A tree house, right there on Weatherby property? But how did it get there, and once it was there, how in the world did anyone get up to it? As far as Harleigh could see, there was no way to get up that wide trunk unless you had a ladder or . . . *Unless you flew,* he found himself thinking, but not believing, of course. Not for a minute.

"Yeah, sure." He snorted, and turned to walk away. Then he turned back to once again stare at whatever it was that had been built way up there in the big old tree. He was still staring when, just above the section of wall, something appeared and then disappeared so quickly he wasn't sure he'd actually seen it. A hairy brown something that might have been—an animal, perhaps a squirrel? Or else . . . And then there it was again, the same mop of dusty-brown hair and beneath it, two eyes. And then a whispery voice called, "Here I am, Harleigh. Up here."

# Chapter Four

At the sudden appearance of the trespasser, Harleigh Four was confused by a series of rapidly changing reactions. The first and most unexpected was a rush of eager excitement. Almost as if he were about to say something stupid like, "Hey! You did come back. I was afraid you wouldn't."

But he managed to bite his tongue and consider some other, more suitable, remarks. Questioning remarks like, "What are you doing up there?" or "Who are you, anyway?" And another one that suddenly seemed especially urgent. "How did you get up there?"

Various possibilities were still shuffling through his mind like a deck of cards when she said, "Do you want to come up?"

Harleigh frowned, gulped, and nodded. "Yes, I guess so. How?"

Her head disappeared behind the piece of wall and then reappeared. "Here," she said. "Get back out of the way." A moment later something fell to the ground at Harleigh's feet with a muffled clanking sound. It turned out to be a bag made of old stiff leather, and inside the bag were three iron rods, each about a foot long.

Harleigh was starting to ask when she explained.

"Look on the trunk of the tree about two feet high. No. More over that way. Do you see a round hole? Push one of those rods into it."

He was about to say he didn't see a hole when he found it, small and round and almost covered by a loose flap of bark. Inside the hole there seemed to be a hollow metal pipe that had been driven into the trunk of the tree. Following the girl's directions, he slid the rod into the pipe until only a few inches remained outside the trunk.

"Now look a little over that way and you'll see another hole. Put another one of the rods in and you can stand on them to reach the hole for the next one," she went on. He followed her directions, but it wasn't easy. Not that he had any trouble figuring out what had to be done. He wasn't stupid. But it was just that even with the two rods firmly in place, it wasn't easy for him to use them to climb up to

where the trespasser was leaning down through a narrow opening between two wooden panels. Even after he realized that there was a another rod already in place farther up, he slipped and had to jump free and start over several times before he reached the point where the girl could grab his arm and help him climb on up. Up to where he was finally able to slide clumsily on his stomach onto a warped and splintery floorboard. Pushing himself to a sitting position, he looked around and quickly decided it was hardly worth the effort.

The planks that formed the floor and walls of the tree house were sturdy but rough and badly stained. Inside the small enclosure there were only a torn and ragged bit of braided rug and a small wooden box, on which sat a rusty tin can full of yellow flowers. Next to the pitiful flower arrangement was a small cup with a missing handle sitting on what was left of a cracked saucer. And overhead—nothing but a piece of ragged canvas.

"Did you build this yourself?" he asked.

"Oh, no." She shook her head solemnly. "I didn't build it. It's been here for years and years. Someone probably built it for some Weatherby children a long time ago. A very long time ago." She pointed. "I found that cup and saucer right down there buried in the dirt near the trunk. I think they're very old. The children they belonged to probably died a long

time ago." She paused thoughtfully before she went on, "I don't think they mind if I use their things."

"How could they mind if they're . . ." Harleigh began and then dropped it. A shiver was crawling down the back of his neck. Hoping to change the subject, he glanced up at the torn canvas roof and asked, "What do you do when it rains?"

She smiled, almost giggled. "Oh, I don't come here when it rains."

"Oh." Harleigh considered for a moment. Considered the fact that he had almost been ready to believe that this was where she lived, right up here in the tree. He shrugged inwardly, excusing himself for having such a stupid idea by thinking that a person could believe almost anything about someone who looked so much like—like what?

Just as before, she was dressed in what seemed to be the ragged remains of a fancy costume, which glittered here and there with all that remained of what must once have been a pattern of shiny sequins. And beneath the sequined tatters, some skin-colored leotards that ended at her wrists and ankles. Her small feet, narrow and long-toed, were bare.

"So, how often do you come here?" he finally asked, and then, before she could answer, "And where do you come *from*? I mean, where do you *live*?"

She didn't answer immediately, but at last she nodded slowly and said, "I've lived in a lot of places. Famous places

like London and New York and Miami. But right now I'm living in Riverbend."

"Well, sure," he said, frowning. "I could have guessed that much. I mean, where in Riverbend."

She sighed and turned her face away. When she looked back, she stared right into Harleigh's eyes. Her own eyes were misty gray and very wide open. "I'm not allowed to say," she said.

"What do you mean? Who won't let you?"

Another mournful sigh. "It's a long story," she began. "My family are very famous people, but they have to be careful because they lead very dangerous lives. So sometimes they send me away to live in Riverbend because they think I'll be safer here."

Harleigh believed her. Or at least he came fairly close to it. He had to swallow hard before he asked, "So you were in danger when you lived with your family?"

"Yes," she said sadly, still staring right into his eyes. "Sometimes I guess I was. I have a very strange story. Maybe I'll tell you someday. But in the meantime, you can call me Allegra."

"Allegra?"

She nodded. "Of course, I have been called other things, but my real name is Allegra. You can call me that."

That did it. He wasn't taking her "being in danger" story

very seriously when he replied, "Okay. I'll call you Allegra, if you promise not to call me Hardly anymore."

She nodded and said she wouldn't. But then she suddenly smiled and leaned forward.

"Tell me about the House," she said. "About Weatherby House."

Pulling his mind back from a lot of unanswered questions, Harleigh shrugged and asked, "Why? What do you want to know about it?"

Her smile widened. "Everything. I really like old houses. All old houses are full of mysteries and stories, and I think the Weatherby House is the most mysterious one in the whole world. I want to know everything about it. Like how many rooms there are and what they all look like. And oh yes, what it looks like right inside those great big front doors. The ones with the carved panels and the big marble posts on each side."

It was Harleigh's turn to smile. "The pillars, you mean. They're called pillars, not posts."

"Yes, pillars," she said eagerly. "They're beautiful."

Harleigh was nodding in agreement when he suddenly wondered how she knew about the pillars, and the doors as well. "Hey," he said. "I guess you haven't spent all your time up in this tree. I mean, how do you know what the front entrance looks like? You can't see it from anywhere outside

our fence. I guess it could be seen from the front gate a long time ago, but not since the trees and bushes got so tall. So you've been sneaking around on Weatherby property?"

Her nod was quick and positive. "Oh, yes. I've been all the way around the House. It takes a long time, but I've been all the way around it."

There was something about the way she said the word "House" that made it seem to need a capital letter. "The House," she said again. "Tell me about the House."

"Well," Harleigh found himself saying, "I really can't say for sure how many rooms there are. I've tried to count them, but I always lose track. But about what's inside those big doors? It's not exactly a room. It's more like a big lobby or entry hall. Right inside those doors, there's this big wide area with fancy antique tables and cabinets and clocks and lots of famous paintings on the walls. There's even"—he tried to make his grin suggest that he thought it was a bit much even for Weatherby House—"there's even a suit of armor. You know, like a whole man made out of pieces of armor. And with a sword and a shield."

She nodded hard. "Yes, I know about medieval suits of armor. I thought there might be one. And what's after that?"

"After what?"

"After the entry hall? What comes next after that?"

So he went on about the drawing room. "It's like an

enormous living room, only nobody lives in it anymore, so all the furniture is covered with dust sheets. And there's this domed ceiling painted with pictures of flying birds and angels sitting on clouds, and things like that. I guess it's all sort of faded, but it still looks pretty good." He was about to start in on the library when she interrupted.

"Now about the people. Not the ones who built it. Tell me about all the people who live there now."

Harleigh was puzzled. He had begun to think he'd figured out what she was about. She was, he'd decided, just another person who loved expensive stuff, particularly if it was *old* expensive stuff. Like the people in Riverbend who pretended to be Aunt Adelaide's friends, but really didn't like her much. People who, as Aunt Adelaide was always saying, only asked her to teas and parties because, even though they knew she'd never accept their invitations, they still thought if they asked her she might ask them to Weatherby House. This girl, Harleigh had decided, was just another person wanting a Weatherby House invitation. But now she was unexpectedly changing the subject to people.

"What about the people?" he asked.

She tipped her head and stared off as if into a far distance. "I don't know," she said at last. "Who they are and what they're like?" Turning back to face Harleigh, she went on, "And the ghosts, too. What are they like?"

"Ghosts? What makes you think there are ghosts in Weatherby House? I've never seen one."

"No?" She sounded incredulous. Unbelieving. "Not even one? Not even the one who walks around on that long balcony sobbing and crying?"

For a moment Harleigh was dumbfounded, but then he laughed. "Oh, that must have been Sheila. She's not a ghost. She's just one of the descendants. Everybody calls her Sad Sheila. Aunt Adelaide says she's hysterical."

"Hysterical?"

"Yes. Whatever that means—besides making her go around looking sorrowful all the time and crying a lot. She came to Weatherby House a long time ago with papers that proved she was related, so Aunt Adelaide let her move in. But most of the other descendants don't like her because they think there must be something funny about the way she descended. Some of them complained about all the noisy crying, so now she goes out onto the balcony to do it."

The girl who called herself Allegra seemed even more fascinated. When Harleigh ran out of things to say about Sheila, she sighed and said, "Oh that's such a sad story. I wish I knew what makes her cry. Don't you know what she's crying about? Haven't you ever asked her?"

Harleigh's answer was simply, "No," but its tone said, *No. Of course not.*

"Oh," Allegra said. Just "oh," but something about the way she said it was definitely disapproving. For a long moment she went on frowning, but then suddenly she stood up. "I have to go now," she said. "But next time I want to hear more about Sheila and the others. All the others. And about the House, too."

She left then, but not by climbing out and dropping off the limb. This time she used the iron rods to climb down to where she waited, calling instructions until Harleigh was back on the ground. Then she pulled out the three lower rods, put them in the bag, and tossed them back up into the tree house. And when Harleigh asked her why she did that, she said, "So no one else will use them."

"So how will you get up the next time you come?"

Her eyes were wide and solemn as she said, "Oh, I don't need them."

Harleigh was still staring up at the tree house wondering about that when there was a rustling noise in the bamboo patch, and when he whirled around she was gone.

# Chapter Five

The next day Harleigh managed to finish his schoolwork almost as fast as the day before, but when he arrived at the tree house no one was there. There was no answer when he called. Not when he shouted, "Hey. Are you up there?" and still nothing a little later when he even went so far as to call, "Allegra. Where are you?"

He waited a while longer, walking around the thick trunk, getting more and more furious at Uncle Edgar for not letting him go sooner. The fourth iron rod was still in place. Still there, but way up out of reach. At least out of his reach. The longer he waited, the more upset he became.

He was mad at Uncle Edgar for making him late, but he

was also angry with the Allegra person. She had said she'd be there, hadn't she? She definitely had said something about "next time." He was sure about that. And "next time" yesterday obviously meant today, didn't it?

On the other hand, he was mad at himself, too. When you came right down to it, what did he think he was doing? Here he was, a direct-descendant Weatherby, running half a mile through berry brambles and bamboo thickets to wait around for a sneaky trespasser to show up. A trespasser who had no business being on Weatherby property in the first place. And who would definitely be told that, in so many words, if she ever showed her face again.

He meant it. And when she did show up a few minutes later, he did tell her so. "Look here," he managed to say, after gulping down his surprise when he turned his head and suddenly there she was. "I guess you know you're breaking the law prowling around on Weatherby property. If Aunt Adelaide or any of the other descendants saw you, the first thing they'd do is call the police. You're already here this time, but this had better be the end of it."

"You mean I can't come here ever again?" she asked in a strangely calm tone of voice, almost as if she didn't believe that he meant what he was saying.

"That's right," Harleigh said sternly, and then began to add, "I mean, not unless—not unless . . ."

But she wasn't listening anyway. Instead she turned and, walking to the big bare trunk, stood staring up toward the tree house. She was smiling when she looked back at Harleigh over her shoulder. "Want to see how I do it?" she asked.

Harleigh stuttered to a stop and then went on, "You mean how you . . . ?" At least he didn't go on and say "fly." And of course she didn't fly, at least not exactly. Instead, she suddenly jumped way up to grab the fourth rod in both hands and then somehow went on up. Her bare feet with their long toes scrambled up the trunk, and her thin, limber body curled and straightened out. Then one of her arms was across the edge of the tree house floor, and a moment later she was leaning out and the bag that held the other rods was landing with a thud at Harleigh's feet.

When the three lower rods were firmly in place, Harleigh managed to join Allegra in the tree house—a little more efficiently this time—and once there, just like last time, there was nothing to do but talk. But somehow, even with all the talking they did that day, Harleigh never did get around to saying anything more about what might happen to people who kept trespassing on Weatherby property.

The first subject that Harleigh brought up was the maze. "I've been looking for a maze," he told Allegra. "You know. A complicated pathway through a bunch of prickly hedges. There's supposed to be one on the Weatherby

property. I've even seen pictures of it, but so far I haven't been able to find it. Do you know where it is?"

She nodded eagerly. "Oh, yes," she said. "We went right past one side of it the other day. You know, where it looks like a high thick hedge. The entrance is right near there, but it's pretty much covered up. But I know how to get in."

"You do?" Harleigh tried not to seem excited. "Could you show me?"

She nodded. "All right. But not right away. I want to talk some more first. Don't you?"

Harleigh didn't. "About what?" he asked, and she didn't say, but strangely enough, that turned out to be the day that Harleigh actually told her about his parents—something that he never talked about, not to anybody. Not even to Uncle Edgar, who apparently had read a book that said that it was healthy for kids to talk about problems they had with other people, particularly their parents. Not that Harleigh Four's parents were that much of a problem. Particularly not his mother, who had died a few days after he was born. And actually, his father wasn't around enough to be that much of a problem either.

"And your father?" Allegra had asked after Harleigh told her about his mother. "Is he dead too?"

"No, of course not," Harleigh told her. "It's just that he's an architect. You know, a person who designs buildings.

Most of the time he's traveling around the world studying famous buildings."

Allegra seemed fascinated. "You mean famous old buildings, like the Parthenon and the pyramids? And then he designs new buildings that are going to become famous too?"

"Famous buildings? My father?" Harleigh did his most negative snort. "That's great! I mean it would be great if his buildings were famous. He's designed a lot of stuff, but most of it hasn't been built."

"Oh." Allegra looked disappointed. "Why don't they get built?"

Harleigh shrugged. "I don't know. Aunt Adelaide says it's because he doesn't have any social skills. He doesn't get along with people. Especially the kind of people who might hire him as an architect. He usually tells people who are thinking about building something that all of *their* ideas are stupid."

Allegra nodded. She thought for a moment before she went on. "And what does he say about you? What does he say about your ideas?"

Harleigh stifled a snort and then a shrug, and managed a grin instead. "Not much," he said. "At least not to me. I guess he talks about me some to Aunt Adelaide and Uncle Edgar; at least they say he does. But when I'm around he says, 'Hello, son' and pats me on the shoulder, and—and that's about it."

Harleigh hadn't meant the words "and that's about it" to mean anything special. He hadn't meant, for instance, that he wished his father would talk to him more. But after he said it, he could tell by the expression on Allegra's face that she thought he might be feeling that way, and that maybe she was feeling sorry for him. It was then that Harleigh told her it was her turn to talk. "So tell me about *your* parents," he said.

She shook her head. "I told you," she said calmly, "sometimes they do things they think are too dangerous for me. I could if they'd let me, but they won't. So sometimes they leave me here in Riverbend." She sighed, stared sadly into space, and then suddenly smiled. "But I want to talk some more about the people you live with. You know, the other people who live in the House."

Harleigh's shrug suggested that he didn't think much of that idea.

"Why?" he asked. "I mean, they're a pretty uninteresting bunch."

"Oh, no. They're all very interesting, and some of them do fascinating things. Like the man with no hair on top of his head who sits out in the courtyard sometimes with a big notebook in his lap. Who is he?"

Harleigh sighed before he began, "Oh, that's Cousin Alden, the writer. He's especially boring. He's Cousin Josephine's husband. I told you about her. She's the one

who takes care of Aunt Adelaide. Uncle Edgar says it's a good thing Josephine gets paid to be Aunt Adelaide's nurse, because nobody ever pays Uncle Alden for anything."

Allegra nodded thoughtfully. "That's too bad. And the one named Sheila who walks up and down the balcony crying."

Harleigh sighed again. "I already told you about her."

"Yes, I know. But not very much. I want to know more about her story." Allegra nodded again. "And then there's the man who goes around waving a big iron wandlike thing over the ground. I think it's a metal detector."

That one was a complete surprise to Harleigh. "A metal detector? I don't know anything about that. What does he look like?"

Her eyes widened as if with fright. "He looks huge—like a giant." She paused then and twisted her mouth into a sort of snarl. "He looks like this." She snarled again. "He has a crooked nose and mean eyes. Really mean eyes. I think he looks scary."

The word "huge" as well as the crooked nose put Harleigh on the right track. "That must be Cousin Junior. He calls himself Junior Weatherby, but Aunt Adelaide says his last name is really something else. He got a lawyer to prove that his mother was a distant relative, so he gets to live in the house, but Aunt Adelaide put him way out in an

ell off the west wing. I guess he didn't like that much. He kept saying he belongs in something better, like on the second floor of the main building, but arguing didn't get him anywhere. Not with Aunt Adelaide."

It was interesting that Allegra thought Junior looked scary because, now that she'd mentioned it, Harleigh realized that he'd always felt pretty much the same way. Especially since the day when he'd been exploring one of the deserted wings of Weatherby House and had suddenly found himself face-to-face with Junior in a dimly lit hallway.

Not that Cousin Junior had tried to hurt him. In fact, all he did was stick out a huge, fat-fingered hand, show his teeth in what was something like a smile, and say, "Hello, Harleigh Weatherby the Fourth" in a slimy tone of voice. It was the smile that was the most frightening. But it was then, remembering that greedy smile, that it suddenly occurred to Harleigh why Junior might have a metal detector.

"I'll bet he was looking for buried treasure," he told Allegra. "There's always been this rumor that there's some sort of treasure buried somewhere on the property. Junior was probably looking for it."

"Buried treasure? What kind of treasure?" Allegra looked delighted.

"I don't know. I guess it was just that people thought Harleigh the First had so much money he must have run

out of places to put it. Something like that. Aunt Adelaide says she never believed there was any treasure, because she knew that a lot of Weatherbys looked for it years and years ago, in every possible place, without finding a thing."

Allegra shrugged and changed the subject. "Now the House," she said. "I want to talk about the House."

Harleigh groaned. "I told you all about it. What more do you want to know?"

Her eyes went wide and glowing. "When can I see it? When can we go inside? I can come here again on Monday. Could I see it then?"

"Look," Harleigh said firmly, "there's no way I can take you inside Weatherby House. Aunt Adelaide would have a fit, and so would all the rest of them. They'd call the police right away, and I might get . . ."

"You might get what?"

He shrugged. "I don't know," he said, but actually he did. At least he had a pretty good idea. He might get sent away to a place called the Hardacre Military Academy, which was something Aunt Adelaide had threatened to do more than once when she thought he'd disobeyed an order.

"Why would they care?" Allegra said. "I wouldn't touch anything. I'd just look."

"Well, Aunt Adelaide would care because she has this very strict rule that nobody, none of the Weatherbys, can

bring anyone into the house without getting her permission first."

"Why does she have a rule like that?"

"She says it's because of the insurance. She says her insurance on the house would be a lot more expensive if any of us let people in when she didn't know about it." Uncle Edgar had said that Aunt Adelaide's insurance excuse wasn't exactly the truth, but Harleigh decided not to go into that at the moment. Actually, he was getting bored with the whole conversation. "So here's a why for *you*," he said. "Why are you so crazy to see it? It's just a big old house."

"I know." Her eyes had a faraway stare as she went on. "I told you. I just like old houses. Houses have mysterious stories. All of them do, unless they're brand-new. And very old ones like Weatherby House have the most."

The one question Harleigh still wanted to ask was what she meant by mysterious stories, but instead he just sighed and said, "Look. It's not going to happen. So just forget about it. Okay? Let's go look at the maze."

Allegra shook her head. "Not today," she said. "Maybe next Monday."

# Chapter Six

It was on the next Monday that Harleigh had a discussion with Uncle Edgar about why they were still having school every weekday, even though all the other schools in the whole country, probably in the whole world, were shut down for summer vacation.

The discussion happened just after Harleigh arrived in the library, where Uncle Edgar had settled himself down at his favorite table behind a big stack of books. After listening to Harleigh's argument, he nodded his big head and said that one important reason was that their study schedule had been arranged by Adelaide the Great.

"And another, slightly more reasonable reason might be that when all those other schools are in session, they

have classes that last all day long. And our little mental workouts"—Uncle Edgar was obviously trying to make a joke of it, pretending to be exercising, raising his big arms up and down lifting imaginary dumbbells—"our little workouts seldom last more than two or three hours. Particularly lately. Lately we haven't been spending even that much time hitting the books."

"Yes, I know," Harleigh said. "But you said that I'd been learning a lot better and faster lately. You did, didn't you? You told me that I'd been finishing lessons in just a few hours that you'd thought would last at least a week. Didn't you? So why should I have to sit around for weeks learning stuff just because a less intelligent student would need that long to learn it?"

Uncle Edgar's grin had a teasing tilt to it that Harleigh didn't appreciate as he said, "And I take it you're saying that we're discussing a student who's bigger and better than average. In every possible way?"

Harleigh gritted his teeth and stared at his tutor through half-closed eyes. Uncle Edgar knew, or he ought to know, how Harleigh hated any mention of his size. If that was what he was hinting about when he said "bigger and better than average," he, Harleigh Weatherby the Fourth, was going to walk out of the room and slam the door and never spend another hour with that stupid old man. . . .

But then, on second thought, he realized that the teasing probably had something to do with his own comment about "less intelligent students." With how he, Harleigh, had made it clear that he considered himself to be a lot more intelligent than any ordinary twelve-year-old. Which of course was true, but maybe it did sound a little boastful to come right out and say so. So Harleigh cooled down and went back to asking if they couldn't have all summer off, like other schools.

Uncle Edgar nodded slowly, "Well, you know it's not up to me. You'll have to speak to Adelaide the Great about it. And good luck. I think you'll need it."

Harleigh knew that was the truth. And he also knew that Uncle Edgar and most of the other descendants resented the way Aunt Adelaide ran everything and made all the decisions. But Harleigh didn't feel that way. At least not always. What he thought was that Aunt Adelaide controlled everything because she couldn't help it. Because as a direct-descendant Weatherby, she was born to be that way. And what he also thought was that he, Harleigh Four, was going to be the same kind of person. And someday he was going to be the one who made all the decisions about what went on in Weatherby House, as well as about even more important things.

"I guess I'll go ask her right now," he told Uncle Edgar. "Okay?"

Shrugging heavily, Uncle Edgar said, "Suit yourself."

Harleigh didn't have far to go. Most of the bedrooms at Weatherby House were on the second and third floors, but because of her wheelchair Aunt Adelaide had long ago chosen a room on the main floor. A huge room that had once been an auditorium, or as Aunt Adelaide called it, the "recital hall."

According to Aunt Adelaide, the homes of very important people always used to have recital halls so they could have entertainments (plays and concerts and solo performances) for their friends. But now the recital hall at Weatherby House was just Aunt Adelaide's bedroom. An enormous room packed full of the best and most valuable Weatherby antiques—not only the huge canopied bed where Aunt Adelaide slept, but also many other especially old and valuable pieces of furniture.

At one end of the long, narrow room there was a raised and curtained-off area that had once been a stage where people had sung and danced and played musical instruments. A stage where the curtains had been closed for many years and where (he'd peeked once or twice) there was nothing to see but a lot of dust and a couple of old pianos.

When Harleigh Four entered the room that morning, Aunt Adelaide was sitting in her wheelchair pulled up to a large table covered with important-looking papers. She was wearing a robe made of purple velvet, and her long

gray hair was tucked up in a matching purple cap. There was no sign of Cousin Josephine, but Harleigh knew she had to be close enough to hear if Aunt Adelaide rang her bell.

"Well, well, Harleigh Four," Aunt Adelaide said, "to what do I owe this visit? An unsummoned visit? You must want something. What is it that you want?" Aunt Adelaide's smile was showing all her long white teeth. But Harleigh knew her well enough to know that her smiles didn't always mean that she was in a friendly frame of mind.

"What I came to ask you . . . ," he began, and then started over. "I was wondering if . . ."

"Yes. Yes. Do go on, child," Aunt Adelaide interrupted impatiently.

Harleigh stuck out his chin, narrowed his eyes, and demanded, "Why can't I have summers off, like people who go to real schools?"

There was no immediate answer. Instead, Aunt Adelaide met Harleigh's stare with one of her own. The famous rock-hard Weatherby stare that Uncle Edgar said could turn Vesuvius into a glacier.

But Harleigh stared right back, and after what seemed like a fairly endless standoff Aunt Adelaide asked, "And what does Edgar say about this idea?"

Without blinking or hesitating, Harleigh answered, "He said I'd have to ask you. So I am."

She nodded. "Yes, so you are. And that does sounds like your Uncle Edgar. Letting someone else do his fighting for him." And then Aunt Adelaide's steely eyes met Harleigh's again, and to his surprise she said, "All right. You've won your case for more vacation time. For the rest of the summer you may have two more free days per week. Say, Mondays and Wednesdays? You may go now and tell Edgar the good news. I'm sure he'll be delighted."

If Uncle Edgar was delighted, he didn't say so. But what he did say was that he was surprised—at least on the one hand. "On the other," he said, "I'm not surprised that *you* were the one who was able to pull it off. What it comes down to is the fact that you're almost as hardheaded as she is."

Harleigh didn't think Uncle Edgar meant that as a compliment, but he took it as one. He was definitely planning to be as hardheaded and powerful as Aunt Adelaide and Harleigh the First combined, and the things he would do would be a lot bigger and more important. He hadn't quite decided what those things would be, but he was working on it, and he knew it would happen. And when it did, that would show all the people who had such a good time laughing at him because of his size. He was planning to show

them all. All the people at Riverbend School and here in Weatherby House, too. That was definitely what he was going to do someday. But right at the moment, what he was intending to do was to leave Weatherby House and head for the black walnut tree as fast as he could go.

# Chapter Seven

It was still quite early when Harleigh arrived at the black walnut tree that day. Allegra wasn't there yet, so he sat down to wait. He sat with his back against the trunk of the tree and wondered whether she really knew how to find the entrance to the maze, and whether she would show him how to get there. After a while he picked up a stick and poked at the rough ground between the roots of the tree and thought about the cup and saucer Allegra had found there, and what she'd said about the children who had once owned them.

He remembered hearing Aunt Adelaide say that there had once been lots of children at Weatherby House, Harleigh the First's children, most of whom had died

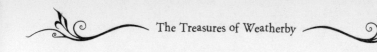

young. So Allegra was probably right when she guessed that the tree house had been built for children who had died many years ago.

He stopped poking with the stick and listened to the silence, thinking about how far he was from Weatherby House and Riverbend and everywhere else in the world where you could hear normal sounds and noises. It was always quiet in the overgrown, deserted Weatherby gardens, but today seemed even quieter than usual. No sounds at all. No breezy whisper among the branches of the tree, and not even the faintest echo of traffic noises from the distant avenue.

And yet . . . and yet, Harleigh was beginning to hear—or imagine he was hearing—something. From a faint, high-pitched murmur it gradually changed to something like faraway singing. Like someone in the far distance singing a children's song. A song that sounded a lot like something that Alice, one of his nursemaids, used to sing to him at bedtime. He remembered Alice saying it was an old song she had sung when she was a little girl. Old enough, he wondered, that it might have been sung by the children who had once played in the tree house?

He was on his feet, his back pressed against the tree trunk, his eyes darting from side to side, when the strange haunting song became a rustling noise that seemed to come

from the direction of the bamboo thicket. The rustle grew louder and came closer, the bamboo thrashed and parted—and Allegra appeared. She looked the same as before, barefooted and dressed in her ragged gown, but she wasn't singing. Not anymore at least.

Harleigh took a deep breath and then had to bite his tongue. What he really wanted to do was to let her know he was angry, except he couldn't think of a way to explain why. So all he said was, "Where have you been? I've been here for a long time."

"Oh, I'm sorry," Allegra said. "Am I late?"

He glanced at his watch and said—nothing, because actually she wasn't. He was early. But in the meantime she had turned away, jumped to grab the top metal handhold, and started scrambling her way up. When the other rods were in place and Harleigh had joined her in the tree house (he was getting better at the climb), he was the first to speak. He began by telling her about his new summer schedule and then, before she had finished agreeing to be there early on Mondays and Wednesdays, he interrupted to say, "And now it's my turn to ask a question. When are you going to show me the maze?"

Her smile was teasing. "Soon," she said. "Just as soon as you promise to show me Weatherby House."

Harleigh glared. He was getting to his feet, pretending to

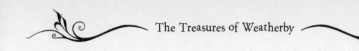
be leaving, when she reached up to tug at his pant leg. "Don't go," she said. "I didn't mean it. When do you want to see it?"

"Right now," Harleigh said.

Actually, it wasn't far away. This time they followed a path that led through another bamboo thicket, but in a different direction, and came out into a grove of saplings where the going was easier and there was more light. Then, just as the forest closed in again and the light dimmed, Allegra stopped and pointed to a place where a fir tree had collapsed against what seemed to be a high prickly hedge.

"It starts here," she said. "Those thick hedges are the beginning of the maze. From here they curve around and just keep on going."

"So those are yew trees." Harleigh felt excited. "They were sent here from England a long time ago. I've heard about them and seen them in pictures, but I didn't know what they looked like up close." He moved closer to touch the stiff green branches with their hard prickly leaves and to stare up at the solid hedgelike wall. "I've been past here before, but I wasn't sure it was part of the maze. I thought it might be, but I couldn't find the way in."

Allegra nodded. "It's not easy to find the entrance. It's hidden by that dead tree. I'll show you where." Pulling back a branch of the fallen fir, she ducked under it and

disappeared. Harleigh followed her, and a moment later he was standing at the beginning of a path that led between two towering green walls. The passageway was tunnel-like, narrow, and not very high.

"It was completely overgrown," Allegra said. "I wanted to open it clear up to the sky, but I can't reach up that high. And then my shears broke when there was still a long way to go. Come on, I'll show you. And be careful. Yews are scratchy."

The narrow tunnel continued for several yards before it turned a corner and split in two. "This way," Allegra said. "That turnoff leads to one of the dead ends. I went that way first and wasted a lot of time. It just curves around and comes back into the main passageway."

Farther along, the tunnel split once more before it suddenly dead-ended. Even near the ground, untrimmed branches of yew reached toward each other from each side, blocking any further progress. "This is as far as I got before my shears broke," Allegra said.

"Your shears?" Harleigh asked. The only shearing he remembered hearing about was something that happened to sheep.

"You know. A gardener's tool, like great big scissors." She pantomimed cutting with shears. "Do you have a pair?"

"Oh, those things. I don't have any, but I think I know where I could get some."

They went back to the tree house then and spent the rest of the morning talking about the maze. Allegra said she'd wanted to see a real maze ever since she'd first heard about them.

"They're just so mysterious," she said. "Like a huge green puzzle that you can get lost in unless you know its secrets. And then I found it. My own maze, that nobody knew about but me." Her eyes widened even more. "I wanted to learn the way through right away. But the pathway was so overgrown, there were a lot of places I couldn't get through at all. So I decided I'd open it up. I've been working on it for a long time." She shrugged. "But then my shears broke."

Listening to her, Harleigh had mixed feelings. He had to agree that mazes were an especially interesting subject. He'd thought about them for a long time. He'd even read up on the subject in the Weatherby library. But Allegra ought to know better than to call it her own maze.

"Well, I've always known about it," he said. "I've even seen old photographs of what it used to look like. When I started looking for it I couldn't find it. But now that I have, I think I'll just . . ." He paused, considering just what he would do now.

"Yes," she said eagerly. "Now we can finish opening it up together. We can start on Wednesday. Okay?"

So on Wednesday, Harleigh came well-equipped. In a

large, dusty toolroom behind the Weatherby carriage house, he had found all sorts of gardening equipment, including any number of shears, rakes, and handsaws.

But opening up the maze turned out to be a lot more hard physical labor than Harleigh had expected. On that first day, he had a hard time keeping up with Allegra and went home with blistered palms and a lot of stiff muscles. So, starting the next afternoon, after his lesson with Uncle Edgar, he went back and worked at least two hours more all by himself. So that was how it went from then on. On Monday and Wednesday mornings he worked with Allegra, and during the rest of the week as many other hours as he could get away.

It got to be a routine he was very good at. A quick dash through dead gardens, bamboo thickets, and groves of saplings, and he would arrive at the maze scarcely out of breath. After retrieving the tools from their hiding place near the maze entrance, he would start to work, cutting the overgrown branches into small pieces and shoving them under the hedge walls. In only an hour or two the pathway through the maze would be longer by several yards.

Now and then Harleigh did ask himself why he was working so hard, but the only answer he could come up with was that it felt like an important thing to do. He wasn't sure why. It might just be something to do with the size of it.

He'd always preferred big things—like Weatherby House, for instance. But another reason might have to do with the fact that the maze had been such an important part of Weatherby history, so putting it back in shape was one way to start making things the way they used to be.

As the days passed, the maze's tunneled passageway became a lot longer and more complicated, but not any higher. It would have taken a much taller person than either Harleigh or Allegra to accomplish the open-to-the-sky corridor it had once been. And each day it became more of a challenge, as they reached new turns, twists, looping intersections, and dead ends, and had to spend more time memorizing their way back to the entrance. It wasn't easy. There were so many places where you could take a wrong turn.

Another, less important, reason Harleigh liked working on the maze was simply that while they were busy there, Allegra spent less time pestering him about letting her visit the House. She still brought it up now and then, but when she did Harleigh found he could put her off by saying he wanted to finish the maze first. To discover the hidden exit that, in the old days, so few Weatherby guests had been able to find by themselves. Allegra seemed to agree that finding the exit was an important goal, and whenever Harleigh mentioned it she usually stopped begging to see the House and went back to shearing and chopping.

In July the weather turned very hot, but it was shady in the tunneled passageway. Shady, and further dimmed now and then by a shadowy green tinged light that seemed to seep out of the surrounding walls of yew, making nearby things look far away, or sometimes just the opposite. The strange greenish light did have a mysterious feel to it, but when Allegra said it was caused by a ghost passing through, Harleigh snorted.

"Oh, sure," he said. "More Weatherby ghosts. Like the one on the balcony?"

Allegra shook her head. "No," she said. "Not like Sheila. Not as sad as Sheila. But ghosts can get lost in the real world, and I think most of them are sad."

Harleigh didn't know what she was talking about, and he told her so. But there were times when he was alone in the maze when he heard faint echoes that sounded like distant voices. He was pretty sure the sounds came from the wind in the yew trees or maybe from birds. But even so, he did sometimes wonder if there were other things he needed to learn about the maze that might be as important as how to find the way out.

# Chapter Eight

It was on a Monday morning in mid-July that Harleigh arrived at the black walnut a little earlier than usual, but Allegra was already waiting in the tree house. Lately he'd been making the climb on his first try, but for some reason on that particular day he slipped and had to start over twice. By the time he finally scooted up onto the floor of the tree house, he'd banged an elbow and a shin and was not in a very good mood.

Allegra, sitting cross-legged with the tatters of the weird ragged dress smoothed down over her legs, looked relaxed and unruffled.

"Do you always wear that same dress?" Harleigh growled.

Allegra nodded. "Oh, yes. When I come here I do. It's

my forest dress." She ran her hands down over the tatters, smoothing them out. "I had another one, but it wore out."

Harleigh couldn't help grinning, wondering what a worn-out dress would look like if this wasn't one.

When the tattered pieces were carefully arranged, Allegra said, "I have a surprise. Look what I brought." She reached in among the rags and pulled out a little bag that had been hanging from a string around her neck. "See this?" she asked.

"Yes, I see it. What is it?"

"It's like a purse or a pocket. I use it when I want to bring something, so my hands will be free for climbing. This time I brought this candy and—and . . ." She fished around in her little bag again and brought out a wrinkled piece of paper. "And this," she said.

The candy was a chocolate bar. Harleigh really liked candy, but he didn't get it very often because Aunt Adelaide thought chocolate was habit-forming. Allegra broke the bar in two and let him pick which piece he wanted. At first that only added to his frustration, because it was broken so evenly it was hard to decide which one was biggest. And after he'd finally chosen, he was sure he'd made a mistake and picked the small one.

But the chocolate did cheer him up a little, and while they were eating she showed him the piece of paper. It

was a photograph that looked like it had been cut from a magazine, and it seemed to be a picture of the front of a very old building. A building that had a grand entrance with large double doors that were decorated by elaborately carved panels.

"And that picture," he said. "What's that?"

"It's some famous doors on a famous building," Allegra said. "But I brought it because it looks so much like the front doors on your House. On Weatherby House. Don't you think so?"

He didn't think so. Not really. A little bit maybe, but not much. But Allegra was sure they were almost exactly alike. They argued about it for a while and then, suddenly, they were on their way to look at the front doors of Weatherby House and see who was right. Afterward Harleigh didn't really remember agreeing to do it, but somehow there they were, on their way.

Harleigh said, "I don't think we can get to where we can see the doors without anybody seeing us." But Allegra was sure they could.

"Oh, I can," she insisted. "I've done it before. Lots of times. First you have to go through the dead garden where all those beautiful statues are . . ."

"The Italian garden," Harleigh said.

"Oh, is that what it is? Italian, I mean," she said. "Good.

So you go through the Italian garden, and then past some other dead flower beds and around behind that other long building at the end of the driveway."

Harleigh nodded. "The carriage house," he said.

"The carriage house?" She looked delighted. "That building was a carriage house? Then they kept horses there? I thought so. Where are the horses?"

He laughed. "Long gone. Now there's just Aunt Adelaide's old Buick, and down at the end there are some rooms where the grooms used to live. But old Ralph is the only one who lives there now."

"Oh," she said. "The old man with a beard? I've seen him. So that's Ralph? Why does he live out there?"

"He's a gardener, but he's too old to do much gardening, except in the solarium. He works in the solarium every morning, and when Aunt Adelaide wants to go to town he drives the Buick."

She nodded. "And then you can either go under the arch where the driveway comes through to the carriage house, or else all the way around that other part. The dead part of the House."

"Dead?"

"Empty," she said. "No one lives there. Did anyone ever live there?"

"No. Not really. You're right about that. The east wing

was just offices and things like that. It's empty now. Most of it is closed off."

Allegra nodded again. "Dead," she agreed with herself. "It's faster to go through the arch, but it's more dangerous. That's when you have to start being very careful."

"Careful?" Harleigh asked. "About what?"

"About the windows. It's dangerous to be where you can see a window, because if you can see one, someone looking out of the window might be able to see you."

Harleigh didn't think it would be possible to reach the house without being in sight of any windows, and he said so, but Allegra just kept on walking and talking and he did too, planning to go just a little farther before he turned and went back. They had passed the remains of the Italian garden and the English one, too, when Allegra came to a sudden stop at the edge of the long sweep of open land: a dry, barren field that had once been a green lawn where Weatherbys and their guests ate picnics and played croquet. A lawn that, according to Aunt Adelaide, was once as lush and green as any three-hundred-year-old lawn in England.

Allegra was pointing out toward the middle of the open field. "Look," she said. "That's where I saw the big man looking for treasure. Right out there."

Harleigh couldn't believe it. "That's where you saw

Junior using a metal detector? Right out there where anyone could see him?"

She shook her head. "Not very well," she said. "It was after dark."

Harleigh was startled. "You don't mean you come here after dark?"

"Not very often. But once I did when the moon was pretty full. That's when I saw him. I saw this enormous man walking around and around out there swinging that metal thing."

It was an uncomfortable thing to imagine—hiding in the bushes after dark and watching sinister old Junior prowling around with a metal detector only a few yards away from your hiding place. Junior, whose creepy stare and curled lip could make a person's skin crawl even in broad daylight . . .

Frozen momentarily while he dealt with the thought of running into Junior outdoors after dark, it took Harleigh a few seconds to notice that Allegra had moved on. He hurried to catch up, to follow her as she crept along behind a hedge, and from there right through the arch that spanned the drive and connected the central part of the house with the east wing.

Once through the archway, Allegra ducked under the hanging branches of a short, bushy tree. When they crawled

out from under the tree they were right against a wall, a wall in which there were no windows.

Looking up, Harleigh realized where they were—just outside the library, the windowless library. And just beyond the library was the curved bulge that was formed by the first floor of his tall central tower. Still on his hands and knees, Harleigh reached out and tapped the only part of Allegra that he could reach—the heel of her bare foot.

"Hey," he whispered when she looked back. "See that tower? That's where my room is. Way up on the top of that tower."

Allegra turned and crawled back. "You mean you live at the top of that tower?" She craned her neck to stare up—way up. When she turned back, her eyes—more than her eyes, her whole face—seemed to be glowing.

He couldn't help being pleased that she was so impressed. "Sure, that's my room. Up on the top floor. The bottom floor right here is an alcove in the library, and on the second floor it's part of an upstairs sitting room. On the third floor it's just a storeroom. But then, way up two more circular flights of stairs, there's this room with a lot of windows that used to be called the Aerie. Nobody lived there. People only went up for the view. But now it's mine. I sleep there."

"That is so exciting." Allegra was still glowing. "You're

so lucky. Everyone should have a tower to sleep in. I wish I had one."

She sighed again before she turned away and crawled to where she could stick her head out between two branches and look up at the turreted tower silhouetted against the sky. She stared for a long time before she suddenly looked back and whispered, "Come on. We're almost there."

They rounded the base of the library alcove, and there, not far away, was the entrance to Weatherby House, the grand entrance with its elaborately carved and paneled door, a door that was similar but not really the same as the one in Allegra's picture.

"See. They're not the same," Harleigh whispered.

But Allegra whispered back, "Yes, they are. Come on, I'll show you." Ignoring Harleigh's objections, she went on crawling around and under bushes on her way to the front doors.

# Chapter Nine

Harleigh was right about the doors when he said they were not the same as the doors in Allegra's picture, because they weren't. Not exactly. As they crept closer, he was able to point out a number of differences in the bas-relief images that were carved into the panels; for instance, the panel where a lion and a unicorn on the door took the place of a knight on horseback in the picture. He was triumphantly pointing out another difference when suddenly Allegra grabbed his arm and pulled him back behind one of the bushes that lined the path.

"Shh," she said. "Get down. Someone's coming."

Flat on his stomach under a scratchy bush, Harleigh

was beginning to hear a squeak and rattle that sounded alarmingly familiar. Aunt Adelaide's wheelchair!

Of course that was who it had to be. No one else entered the house by way of the front entrance. All the other descendants had keys to other doors—side and back doors—ones that led from the service road to the kitchen, from the courtyard through the solarium, or even into some of the more distant ells and wings of the house. But Adelaide the Great always came and went by way of the grand front entrance.

Both of them would be in serious trouble if they were seen. At least if they were seen together. Of course, Harleigh was in no real danger, as long as he was by himself. But if Aunt Adelaide were to find out that he had someone with him, that he had allowed a stranger to come onto the premises without having permission, there was no telling what might happen. Particularly if he wasn't able to give an explanation—not a believable one, anyway—of how she had managed to get herself onto Weatherby property.

Pushing himself back as far as he could among the prickly leaves, Harleigh glanced at Allegra and saw that she was frightened too. As frightened as he was, or maybe even more so. Her gray eyes looked enormous and her whole face, usually so alive and changeable, was stiff and still.

"Don't worry." Harleigh's whisper was barely louder than a breath of air. "Just stay right there where you are." He began to move then, wiggling backward through the bush to where he could get to his feet at a safe distance from Allegra's hiding place, before he jumped up and burst out onto the path, calling, "Hello, Aunt Adelaide. Hi, Cousin Josephine."

Aunt Adelaide, and Cousin Josephine as well, couldn't have looked more surprised and startled if he'd been wearing armor and brandishing a sword. "Good heavens, child," Josephine said. "You gave me a start. What are you doing way out here?"

Right at first Aunt Adelaide didn't say anything except with her eyes, but what they were saying wasn't particularly reassuring.

"I was just running around," Harleigh said. "Getting some fresh air and sunshine, like the doctors said."

"I see," Aunt Adelaide said. "And do you often play way out here? I thought you were spending your free time in the old gardens in the north acreage."

"Oh, usually I do." Harleigh fell in behind the wheelchair in order to help Josephine push it over the graveled path, as well as to get away from Aunt Adelaide's probing stare. "Here. Let me help," he said, and then added, "Most of the time I stay in the old gardens. But today I

decided to see how long it would take me to get all the way around the house. That's how I happened to be out here."

They had reached the portico by then, and Harleigh helped push the wheelchair up the ramp that led between marble pillars and on up to the huge double doors. When the wheelchair came to a stop, Aunt Adelaide held out a key ring the size of a bread plate, from which dangled at least a half dozen large, old-fashioned keys.

"Well, since you're here you may as well make yourself useful and unlock the door for us," she said. "It's the largest key. The one with the silver crest."

Harleigh knew which key it was. He'd seen it before, but he'd never held it in his hand. He liked the strong solid heft of it as he fitted it into the matching crest just below the lion's-head doorknob. The key grated as it turned, there was a clicking sound, and one of the heavy doors swung open. Dropping the key ring into Aunt Adelaide's outstretched hand, he moved back to help push the chair over the door-sill. Over the sill and then on down the wide entry chamber, beneath crystal chandeliers and ancient oil paintings, past narrow rosewood tables, an enormous pendulum clock, a hexagonal curio cabinet, and last but not least, a complete suit of armor. They had almost reached the pointed arch above the short entry hall that led into the drawing room,

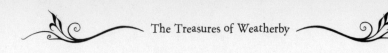

when Aunt Adelaide looked back and said, "The door. Harleigh, I don't think you closed the door tightly. Just push it shut firmly and you will hear it lock itself."

He hadn't heard a click. "I'll get it," he said, and turned back just as Cousin Josephine and the wheelchair disappeared into the drawing room. Running back down the length of the huge entryway, Harleigh was reaching out to close the door, when it suddenly began to move. When he pushed, the door pushed back, and a small hand and bare foot appeared in the crack, quickly followed by the rest of Allegra.

"Get out," Harleigh whispered. "You can't come in here." Putting both hands on her shoulders he pushed—pushed her back against the door, which closed with a loud click. A click that meant there was no way to open it except by using the key on Aunt Adelaide's ring.

"Now you've done it," he hissed. "The door's locked. You can't get out."

She nodded slowly. Her rolling eyes had a wild gleam that might have been fear or—something else.

"Didn't you hear me?" he demanded. "You've locked yourself in."

She turned back to stare directly at Harleigh. "I didn't lock myself in. I just came in. *You* were the one who pushed and made the door lock. Anyway, I'm . . ." She looked around again and began to whisper, "I'm in. I'm in the House."

Harleigh thought fast, or tried to. On the right side, just beyond the grandfather clock, the first door was to the library, where they just possibly might run into Uncle Edgar. And the second was to the servants' hall that passed the pantry and kitchen where—Harleigh glanced at his watch—Matilda might be getting ready to make lunch.

On the left was the entrance to the drawing room, but that was where Aunt Adelaide and Cousin Josephine had just gone. The only other escape route was by way of the wide west corridor that led to Aunt Adelaide's recital hall bedroom—where she would be going as soon as she finished her usual inspection detour through the drawing room.

Aunt Adelaide liked to say she always went through the drawing room because it reminded her of all the splendid events that had taken place there when she was a girl. But other people thought another reason was that Adelaide the Great wanted to check to be sure that no one—no distant descendant—had dared to take, or even touch, anything.

"She usually makes me stop and lift the sheets off the best pieces," Harleigh had heard Cousin Josephine say, "so she can be sure nothing has been disturbed."

So if today's inspection took long enough, there might be time to make it down the west corridor and out through the solarium. He motioned for Allegra to follow him. But she didn't, at least not right away. Instead she went on standing

in the center of the entry hall, turning slowly in a circle—turning and looking and breathing deeply in long, shivery sighs.

"What are you doing?" Harleigh hissed. "Come on." Grabbing her wrist, he pulled her on down the entryway and under the arch that led into the west corridor, but they hadn't gone far when he heard a squeaky creak. One of the side doors that led into the drawing room was opening, which meant that the inspection tour was over and Aunt Adelaide was on her way to the recital hall. There was no time to be choosy. Pulling Allegra after him, Harleigh darted through the nearest door and into a place he had been before, but not often and not at all recently.

# Chapter Ten

It was almost dark. In the dim light the wood-paneled walls gave the room an enclosed cavelike feeling, and the groups of bulky leather-covered chairs resembled clusters of squatting monsters. The dead air smelled like a dirty ashtray. Allegra pulled her arm free. "Where are we?" Her voice was low and shaky.

"We're in one of the men's rooms," Harleigh said, and then, realizing what she might think, he started to explain. "I mean . . ."

"A men's restroom?"

"No. Not a restroom. They're just called the men's rooms because no women were allowed."

Allegra stopped turning in a circle and came back to face Harleigh. "Why not?" She sounded indignant. "Why couldn't women come in here?"

"I don't know." Harleigh tried not to sound argumentative—it wasn't the time or place for a quarrel. "My great-grandfather, Harleigh the First, said so, I suppose. It was only these two rooms. This one used to be called the smoking room and in there, through that door," he said, pointing, "is the poolroom. My aunt says women and girls weren't allowed in there, either."

"And now? Who's allowed in them now?" Allegra was forgetting to keep her voice down.

"Shh," Harleigh cautioned. "No one uses them much anymore. Sometimes my uncle plays pool with me." His voice sank to a whisper. "But I don't think anyone ever comes in here anymore."

Allegra nodded slowly, and once again began to turn in slow circles. "I can see why. I don't like this room. I don't think anything interesting ever happened here." She shuddered. "And it smells bad."

"I know," Harleigh said. "From all the tobacco."

She shook her head. "That too," she said. "But there's a dull feeling. Dull and uninterested."

"You mean uninteresting," he said.

She thought for a moment before she said, "No. I think

I meant uninterested. Can we go? Could I see the pool-room now?"

"See the poolroom?" Harleigh asked sternly. "Look. Forget about seeing things. What we have to do now is get you out of here before someone sees *you*."

That's what he said, but on second thought he realized she would have to see the poolroom, because going through it was the safest way to get to the solarium and from there out into the courtyard. "Well, come on," Harleigh said. "Here it is. Here's the poolroom."

The light in the poolroom was a little better. Once inside, Allegra walked slowly around, reaching out to touch everything she passed: the pool table, the bar, and the surrounding clusters of chairs and stools.

She was running her fingers along the rack of pool sticks when Harleigh demanded impatiently, "Come on. You have to get out of here."

She sighed. "I know. But there's so much more to see. Can't I stay a little longer?"

Watching her reactions, the way any fear or anxiety she might—and certainly should—be feeling seemed to be almost completely forgotten in her fascinated interest in everything, Harleigh found himself wishing that she could stay just a little longer. Long enough for him to find out why seeing the house mattered so much to her. Or maybe

just so he could show her some really grand rooms, like the library and the drawing room. But it just wasn't possible.

"No, you can't." Harleigh tried to sound very firm. "You have to go." At the door that led to the entrance to the solarium he turned back to motion and say, "Come over here. Stand right here by this door while I go check to be sure that the gardener isn't there. And when I come back, follow me and run as fast as you can. Okay?"

She nodded. He was sure of that, and he was pretty sure she whispered, "All right."

After the heavy glass-and-steel door of the solarium closed behind him, Harleigh ran from one side of the greenhouse to the other, stopping only long enough to check out each of the aisles. Just to be sure, he went down one aisle far enough to check behind some big-leafed tropical plants and a dangling curtain of flowering vines. No one was there. No sign of Ralph, the gardener, who should be showing up any time now. But for the moment the coast seemed to be clear.

Relieved, Harleigh dashed back into the hall, reached the poolroom door, jerked it open, and found—no one at all. He couldn't believe it. No one in the poolroom and not, he checked quickly, in the smoking room, either.

His first thought was that she must have been caught. She'd been spotted by one of the descendants and dragged

off to Aunt Adelaide's room, or even to the front gate to be held while someone called the police.

But as he checked both rooms a second time, he began to wonder if the crazy girl had just decided to give him the slip and try to explore Weatherby House all by herself.

The more he thought about it, the more he became certain that that must have been what happened. She'd simply decided to go off sightseeing on her own. And along with that conviction came a surge of anger—more and more of it the longer he thought about how she'd promised she'd wait right there by the door. Promised, and then broken her word.

"Stupid girl," he muttered. "They'll catch her for sure, and then both of us will be in a whole lot of trouble." He had no idea what they'd do to her—jail maybe, or at least juvenile hall. But he was pretty certain it would mean the Hardacre Military Academy for Harleigh J. Weatherby the Fourth. The boarding school that, according to Aunt Adelaide, had "made a man of" other Weatherby boys who'd needed a "little extra push in the right direction."

And from Uncle Edgar, who had been one of those boys, he'd heard what that extra push could do to you. Uncle Edgar's stories were about canings and solitary confinement, as well as bullying older boys who liked to use smaller boys for punching bags. And since he'd previously been threatened with Hardacre Academy for much smaller

sins than sneaking a stranger into Weatherby House, he felt sure that was where he'd be headed if Allegra were caught.

Or else . . . Or else, it suddenly occurred to him, maybe Allegra could be the only one in trouble. All he had to do was go back to his room in the tower and read a book and not come out until they caught her, and then he'd just pretend he knew nothing about it. And when she told them that he'd let her in, he'd simply say he hadn't. Which wouldn't even be a lie, because the truth was that she'd pushed her way in while he was trying to push her out. And after that maybe he'd say he'd never seen her before in his whole life. Which would have been the truth if someone had asked him just a few weeks ago. Too bad for Allegra, but that was how it was going to have to be.

# Chapter Eleven

So that was it. The next step would be to get to his room, where he would wait until he was sure she'd been caught. It wouldn't be a long wait, he was sure of that. One of the descendants—Uncle Edgar on his way to the kitchen for a snack, or Cousin Josephine running an errand for Aunt Adelaide—would be sure to catch sight of the trespasser before many minutes had passed. And then the hunt would be on, and she'd soon be captured.

Peeking out of the smoking room, Harleigh checked up and down the length of the west hall. No one in sight. He slid through the barely opened door and ran on tiptoe. He was in the entry hall and had just passed the knight in armor when a sudden sound startled him, making him break his

stride, trip, and almost fall. He skidded to a stop at the foot
of the wide marble stairway and turned to stare back toward
the place where there'd been a sharp metallic clang. Back to
where the knight stood just as he always had, with one
gloved hand holding his sword and the other resting on the
top of the circular shield that leaned against one of his
ironclad feet. The sound had definitely come from that
direction, but nothing had changed and no one was there.

He went on then, running to the top of the grand stairway, up the second flight to the third floor, and on up the
circular stairway until, a little breathless, he arrived at the door
that led into his own very private Aerie. He stopped for a
moment to look back down the curving iron stairway, where
nothing stirred and the silence was unbroken. He breathed
deeply, clenched his teeth, and strengthened his resolve to
let Allegra pay for her treacherous behavior all by herself.
Then he went in and closed the door firmly behind him.

But it was only a few minutes later, after he had selected
a book, settled himself comfortably on his bed, and was trying to concentrate on what he was reading, when he heard
it. Someone, or something, was knocking softly on his door.

For a startled, almost panicky moment, Harleigh stared
at the door, trying to make himself believe that he had imag-
ined it. The knocks hadn't been all that loud. Maybe it
hadn't been . . .

But then they came again, louder this time. *Knock, knock, knock.* Harleigh got to his feet and walked to the door, slowly turned the knob, and even more slowly opened the door a small crack. And there she was, smiling at him as if everything was just fine. As if she hadn't run away when he'd warned her to stay right where she was until he came back for her.

Doing his fiercest Weatherby glare, Harleigh opened the door barely wide enough for her to squeeze through. But once inside, she forgot all about him. Ignoring his glare and evading his hand as he reached out to grab her, she ran to the closest window. After running her hand along the wide sill, she stood on tiptoe to look out and down. She stared out for a long time before she ran to the next window, and then the next.

It wasn't until she'd completed the whole circle and looked out every window that she turned to Harleigh and began to talk—just as he was starting to tell her what a mess she'd made of everything by not staying where he told her to, and how much trouble they were both in now, and how it was all her fault. When he finished, he wasn't sure she'd heard any of it. Hurrying, almost running, back to the nearest window, she went on with whatever it was she'd been saying until he finally was able to interrupt her by demanding, "How did you find your way

up here, anyway?" And then suddenly he thought he might know. "You were following me, weren't you?"

She nodded, looking pleased, as if he'd just paid her a compliment. "Yes. Yes I was. I think you heard me when I was hiding behind the knight." She smiled, almost giggled. "You almost fell down?"

Harleigh frowned. He didn't see what was so funny about it, and what he really didn't get at all was how anybody could hide behind a skinny knight in armor. "How did you . . . ," he was starting to ask when she explained.

"I was down behind his shield, only I bumped it a little and it hit his shoe. That was what made the noise."

Only that wasn't a real explanation. Not one you could really believe. There was no way anyone could hide behind a shield that wasn't much bigger than a garbage can lid. But then, remembering how Allegra curled and uncurled her skinny little body as she climbed the black walnut tree, he wasn't so sure. She probably had been there all right, folded up like a cat, right behind the knight's shield.

And immediately afterward, she'd somehow managed to follow him up all those flights of stairs without being seen or heard. So now, here she was and there went his plan to let her get caught by herself so he could deny knowing anything about her.

With his hands on his hips, Harleigh rearranged his glare,

making it exactly like the one on Harleigh the First's famous face in the library portrait. "So," he said. "What do you think you're going to do now? The front doors are locked and Aunt Adelaide has the only key. And I'll bet you can't find your way back to the solarium, and even if you did, the gardener's probably there by now. But you have to leave now, right this minute, and I'm not going to . . ."

Even before Harleigh finished with what he was not going to do, Allegra turned away. Running toward the nearest window, she reached for the latch and, rising up on her tiptoes, started to lean forward.

Harleigh stuttered to a stop, fearing . . . or at least wondering . . . But then she pulled her head back in, turned toward him, and said—not what he'd been almost expecting. Nothing about flying, but only, "I think someone stood right here looking out toward the highway, for hours and hours—for years, maybe. I think she was watching for someone to come. But he didn't. Not ever. It was very sad. Do you know who she was?"

Harleigh didn't. And he didn't believe there had ever been such a person—at least he certainly didn't at that particular moment.

# Chapter Twelve

When Allegra made up the story about a person who had looked out the tower window watching for someone to come, Harleigh said, "I've never heard about anything like that. Who was she?"

"I don't know." Allegra's eyes had that unfocused, faraway stare. "I thought maybe you might know about it."

"Well, I don't. The only thing I ever heard about this tower was that the Weatherbys used to bring people up here to look at the view. My aunt says that important people from all over the country wanted to be asked to a Weatherby Sunset."

Allegra nodded vaguely and turned back to walk around the room, running her fingers along the walls and over the

broad windowsills. When she came back, she nodded slowly and sighed before she said, "Yes. Other people came here too." She sighed again before she said, "There are happy stories, but sad ones, too."

For some reason an involuntary shiver lifted Harleigh's shoulders. But he shook it off and said, "Well, there's one sad story I can tell you about, and that's the one about the mess we're both going to be in if someone sees you."

"You too? You'd be in trouble too?"

"I certainly would. I told you about Aunt Adelaide's rule that no one can bring strangers into the house without getting her permission."

Allegra looked concerned. "Would they beat you?"

"No," he said. "What they would do, though, is send me away."

"Oh no!" Allegra said. "They couldn't do that, could they?"

"They could if they wanted to," Harleigh said.

"So how do we get me out without anyone seeing us?" Allegra finally sounded a little worried. But not anywhere near as worried as she ought to be.

Harleigh let his frustration show in the way he said, "I don't *know*. That's what I'm trying to tell you. Maybe if we . . ." He stopped, as he hastily began to go over the possibilities. "Maybe we could go through the kitchen to

the service entrance when Matilda—she's our cook—is in one of the pantries." He shook his head. "But we'd have to be very quiet and fast—and lucky."

There had to be a better way. There was the door just beyond the poolroom that led out into the solarium, but that would be very risky, now that old Ralph would almost certainly be there. If they could get to the library and Uncle Edgar wasn't there, it would be a good place to hide, but it had no outside exit, not even a window. From there the only way out was through the entry hall and the front doors, which, of course, were locked. The only other possibility would be to go all the way down the west corridor to one of the wings that branched off it, and then to a rear entrance that was used by the distant descendants who lived in one of the west wings. That would be dangerous too, especially the first part, where they would have to go down the corridor that went right past Aunt Adelaide's recital hall. But something had to be done, and quickly, and the west hall exit might be the best possibility.

"Come on," he said.

She held back. "To where? Where are we going?"

"Out of the house."

"But how?"

"I'll show you. Just follow me."

At first she did. As they wound their way down the

circular stairway she kept close behind him. But later, on the third-floor landing and again as they made their way across the huge expanse of the ballroom, she insisted on stopping to look one way and then the other. And each time, when Harleigh turned back to urge her to hurry, she seemed to be listening as well as looking. Listening to something—but not to him.

He had to call louder and then even more loudly before she turned toward him, raising her shoulders in a kind of shiver. "All right," she said. "All right. I'm coming."

They were on the grand stairway and nearing the main floor when Harleigh began to hear a frightening sound—the squeal and whirr of Aunt Adelaide's wheelchair. Grabbing Allegra's wrist, he pulled her the rest of the way down the stairs, through the nearest door—and into the library.

Good. It was dark. Very dark. Which meant that Uncle Edgar wasn't there. Shuffling forward carefully, feeling his way, Harleigh reached the nearest lamp. With his fingers on the switch, he stopped to wonder why he was lighting the lamp when complete darkness would be best for hiding. But then he went ahead and flipped the switch and turned quickly to watch Allegra's face when she saw . . . when she, for the first time, saw Harleigh Weatherby the First's magnificent library.

Just as he expected, Allegra seemed to be absolutely

amazed. Looking up at the book-lined walls soaring up to the huge stained-glass dome, Allegra caught her breath and then froze for a moment, as if transformed into a statue. A statue of a small, thin girl in a ragged dress, who stood perfectly still for several seconds before she slowly came out of her paralysis and began to turn in a circle. And then, still without saying a word, she began to move, wandering off between the tables and along the nearest wall. Moving as slowly and uncertainly as a sleepwalker, reaching out to touch everything she passed — the chairs and tables and shelf after shelf of books. Harleigh caught up with her just as she stopped beneath the enormous painting of Harleigh the First in its massive golden frame.

"Well, what do you think?" Harleigh asked, not expecting much more than astonished gasps and wordless wonder.

Allegra smiled and nodded. "It's so big," she said.

"I know." Harleigh was pleased.

She looked at him and smiled. "And you're allowed to read these books? Any book you want?"

"Of course," he said. He made a sweeping gesture. "I've read a lot of them. But how about the place? What do you think of . . ." He gestured grandly. "Of this room?"

"This place?" She nodded, and then said, "It's beautiful, but it's not . . ."

"It's not what?" Harleigh asked suspiciously.

She shook her head. "It's so—quiet. It doesn't have stories. At least not many." She paused, looking around as if searching for a better answer to his question.

"No stories?" He could hardly believe his ears. "It probably has every story that was ever written. At least every one that was written back when it was built."

"I mean . . . ," she said, "I mean, some of the other rooms are full of . . ." She paused again.

"Full of what?" Harleigh said indignantly.

She nodded and then went on uncertainly, "Of stories . . . When you close your eyes and breathe deep you can almost hear them whispering their stories."

She wasn't making any sense. "Well, we're lucky that nobody's whispering stories about you being here. At least not yet."

"I know," she said. "Where are we going now?"

"I don't know. But maybe . . . Wait here." He started away, and then came back. "Wait right here. Don't go anywhere. Okay?"

"Okay," she agreed quickly. Quickly, as if she meant it, but on second thought he changed his mind. He wasn't going to be ditched again. Grabbing her wrist, he said, "No. You come too." At the door to the entry hall he whispered, "Shh" and put his ear to the door.

At first he could still hear the wheelchair, fainter now

and farther away, and then a door slammed and there was no sound at all. Aunt Adelaide had gone either by way of the dining room or else down the service hall on her way to the kitchen.

"Now," Harleigh said to Allegra. "Now's our chance. Follow me."

Now that he knew where Aunt Adelaide was, Harleigh felt sure the safest route would be through the drawing room, since no one else was allowed to go there. Checking to be sure that Allegra was close behind him, he led the way—under the grand arch and on into the huge drawing room, under clusters of sparkling chandeliers, and below enormous oil paintings in elaborate gilded frames. He walked quickly and quietly, and at first Allegra stayed beside him. But when he stopped to listen for footsteps or the sound of the wheelchair, he found that she was once again wandering off.

Moving lightly and quickly, she was halfway across the room before he caught up with her. "What do you think you're doing?" he hissed, but when she turned to face him, she was smiling.

"I'm listening. Can't we stay here just a little while?"

"Are you crazy?" He once again grabbed her wrist, and this time he didn't turn it loose. When he reached the door to the west corridor he peered out.

No one was in sight. The wide corridor that led to the one-time recital hall was empty and quiet. He silently congratulated himself for choosing the right escape route. With Allegra still in tow, they had passed the double doors that led into Aunt Adelaide's recital hall bedroom when Allegra came to an abrupt stop.

"Listen," she whispered. "I hear something."

"Where?"

"In there." She was pointing to the small door they had just passed, a door that had been locked for years, but that had once been used by performers on their way to the recital hall's stage.

"There's nothing in there except some stairs that go up onto the stage," Harleigh said. "Nobody's there. Nobody's been up there for years and years."

Harleigh was still talking, shaking his head and talking, when he suddenly thought he was hearing something too. Or perhaps only imagining a faint beeping sound that seemed to be coming from behind the door. He ran, pulling Allegra behind him.

After making the turn into one of the west wing ells, and continuing on into a small entry vestibule, they reached their destination. Harleigh slid to a stop. Directly in front of them was the exit he'd been headed for. He tried the door and it was unlocked. No one was in sight.

He'd done it. He'd gotten Allegra out of Weatherby House, and he was pretty sure no one had seen her. He was pushing her toward the door when she suddenly dodged away from him and came to a stop. "It was that same man," she whispered urgently. "The one with the metal detector."

Harleigh was confused. "What man are you talking about? Where?"

"Behind that stage door. I heard him. I heard his detector thing."

"What? Who?" Harleigh was still stammering when she spun away and, running so fast he knew he could never catch her, disappeared into the Weatherby jungle.

# Chapter Thirteen

Harleigh was really angry. Every time he thought about what Allegra had done, he got angrier. He kept reminding himself how she had started the whole dangerous mess by squeezing in the door when he was trying to push it shut. But what made him even more teeth-grindingly furious was how she had run off and hid when he'd told her to stay right there by the solarium door and wait for him to come back. And then, when the whole scary mess was almost over and they'd finally made it to a west wing exit, she'd made up a fantastic lie for no reason at all. He had no idea why she'd said what she did, except maybe to be sure he'd come looking for her as soon as he could, to find out what on Earth she'd been talking about.

So he wasn't going to do it. Even on Wednesday morning, he decided, he was just going to stay home where, when people lied to him, at least he knew why.

The thing was, he didn't believe any part of what Allegra had said. It just wasn't possible that Junior Weatherby could have been in Aunt Adelaide's recital hall with a metal detector, and even if he had been there, there was no way Allegra could have known about it. She certainly hadn't seen Junior, and as for hearing something . . . Harleigh was sure now that he hadn't heard anything, and that meant she hadn't either.

So when Wednesday morning arrived, Harleigh didn't even think about going to the tree house and then, as usual, to work on the maze. For one thing, it was a dark and gloomy day. The clouds that drifted over Weatherby House hung so low that all the towers were wrapped in a drifting gray veil that formed and reformed in strangely threatening shapes, shapes that resembled dragons or huge hands with clutching fingers. The clouds were definitely threatening—rain or perhaps something even worse.

He was still brooding about what Allegra had done on his way down to breakfast. He was going over every part of it and getting even angrier when, slamming through the kitchen door, he ran into someone carrying a cup of coffee. The person wiping spilled coffee off his jacket was Harleigh J. Weatherby the Third, Harleigh Four's father, whom he

hadn't seen for almost six months. After he got a towel and wiped himself off, Harleigh the Third put his hand on Harleigh Four's shoulder and said, "Hello, son."

Harleigh said hello, and then, "Here, I can do that." While he went to get another towel to mop up the floor, his father went back to telling Aunt Adelaide and Uncle Edgar and Cousin Josephine about how bad the weather had been in New York and how the airline had lost his luggage in Chicago.

Breakfast was over before his father looked at Harleigh and said, "So, I hear you've moved into the central tower and that you've been making very good progress in your studies." Then he put both hands on Harleigh's shoulders and stared at him as he said, "Well done, son." And then, after a moment, he went on, "And you *have* been growing. Haven't you?"

Harleigh Four knew what his father meant when he stressed the word "have." What "You *have* been growing, haven't you?" meant was that *his father had been right* in urging Harleigh to have that last operation. The one that not only his father, but a lot of doctors, too, had insisted would solve the problem with his heart so that, when he recovered from the operation, he would finally start to grow. Only Harleigh Four had been sure they were lying to him again, and he'd been right. The last time he'd measured himself,

which hadn't been all that long ago, he'd been about the same as ever.

So when his father said he'd been growing, Harleigh's only answer was, "Oh, you think so?" in a tone of voice that said he didn't believe it for a minute. Or would have, if anyone had been listening.

It wasn't until after Harleigh the Third had gone off with Uncle Edgar that anyone else had anything to say to Harleigh Four. This time it was Aunt Adelaide. He had just taken his dirty dishes to Matilda and was heading for the door when he heard his great-aunt's creaky voice calling his name. Turning back, he asked, "Did you call me?"

"Yes, I did." She rolled her chair a little bit closer, and her steely eyes got even more metallic. "I just wanted to ask if you've been in my room lately."

"Lately?" He tried to think back. "Well, the last time must have been when I came in to ask about . . ." He'd gotten that far when a shocking idea occurred to him. Did she mean had he been there when she wasn't there? And if she did, what made her think he, or at least someone, had been there? After a speechless moment, he went on, "I mean, the last time must have been when I came to ask you if I could have more days off for summer vacation." But by then he was sure there was more to it than that. Looking right into her knife-sharp gray eyes, he asked, "Did you mean when you weren't there?"

"Yes, as a matter of fact, I did. Have you?"

Without blinking, Harleigh said, "No, I haven't. Why did you ask me that?"

Great-Aunt Adelaide's famous Weatherby stare went on for a long time while Harleigh forced himself to stare back, until at last she nodded slowly. "I am asking you because the recital hall has recently had an uninvited visitor who rummaged around in my personal possessions and caused some serious damage. And it occurred to me and your Cousin Josephine as well that it must have been you."

"No. It wasn't me. It wasn't," Harleigh said, but Aunt Adelaide only turned her chair away and called to Cousin Josephine, who had been talking to Matilda.

And that was the end of it, except it wasn't, really. Not the end of it for Harleigh, who knew he hadn't been the one, and so was left to wonder who might have been in Aunt Adelaide's room, and what that person had been doing there. And most of all, whether or not this new mystery had anything to do with what Allegra said she'd heard. That was the most important question—whether it meant that Allegra might have been telling the truth after all, and really had heard someone on the stage of the recital hall while Aunt Adelaide had been somewhere else in the house.

A little later, back in his tower room with the blinds pulled to shut out the damp gray ooze of fog, Harleigh tried

to get his mind on the book he'd been reading and off the subject of who might have been in Aunt Adelaide's room. He didn't realize that he had worked himself up into a jumpy frame of mind, but when there was a sudden loud knock on his door, he jumped so hard he dropped his book.

After he'd gulped and gulped again and finally managed to ask who it was, the door opened. It turned out it to be only his father, who came in, mumbled hello, and looked around for quite a while before he said, "But there isn't a closet."

"I know," Harleigh said. "I don't mind."

"But you should have a closet," Harleigh the Third said. "I'll see to it."

"Those cabinets hold most of my stuff, and there are lots of big armoires on the third floor," Harleigh Four said. "It would be a lot easier to move one of them up here."

His father shook his head. "No, a real closet, I think." He walked around the room, stepping over some piles of books and pushing other things out of his way. He stopped once or twice to squint his eyes and sight over his thumb before he said, "Yes, a closet is possible. I'll draw up some plans."

Harleigh Four was sure that he would. His father was very good at drawing up plans. But that probably was as far as it would go. Harleigh didn't mind. He was used to being without a closet.

After his father left, Harleigh went back to trying to keep his mind on his book, but before long he gave up on reading and began instead to make plans of his own. Only his weren't about things that might or might not get built. What he was planning was how he might find out who had been in Aunt Adelaide's room, and what that person had done while he was there.

The first step might have to be a talk with Cousin Josephine, who apparently had told Aunt Adelaide that she thought he, Harleigh Four, might have done it—whatever *it* was.

Finding a way to talk to Cousin Josephine when she was alone might not be easy, but that definitely had to come first. It might be difficult because Cousin Josephine was almost always with Aunt Adelaide, either pushing her wheelchair or taking care of her in other ways. However, Cousin Josephine actually lived in a suite of rooms on the second floor with her husband, Cousin Alden, so she must go up there sometimes. If Harleigh could figure out when she went there, and what route she took, he might have a chance to talk to her when she was alone.

Using a Sherlock Holmes–type process of elimination, Harleigh began to rule out certain times of day, the times when Cousin Josephine was always with Aunt Adelaide— getting her up in the morning and taking her to meals. And

after that there was putting her to bed at night. That left a few hours in the afternoon, which might offer a possibility. But an even better one might be in the evening after she'd put Aunt Adelaide to bed. Harleigh had heard Aunt Adelaide say that she was always in bed by nine o'clock. So that, he decided, was the best bet.

Now the time was decided on, and the place would have to be somewhere along the shortest route between Aunt Adelaide's recital hall bedroom and Cousin Josephine's suite.

It wasn't difficult to pick out a likely spot. So it was that same evening around nine o'clock that Harleigh Four, book in hand, settled down on an ornate Chinese chest near the top of the first flight of the grand staircase to wait for Cousin Josephine to pass by.

# Chapter Fourteen

Sitting cross-legged on the Chinese chest, Harleigh opened *Great Expectations* to his favorite part—where Pip visits Miss Havisham's disgusting, rat-infested mansion—and settled himself to read and wait. But the only light, which came from widely spaced crystal chandeliers in which only a few ancient bulbs were still burning, was very dim. He squinted his eyes and tried, but the printed words soon faded away to meaningless blurs. Closing the book, he leaned his head back against the wall.

It was later, maybe only a few minutes, or perhaps quite a while, when he suddenly sat upright. Shaking his head and blinking his eyes, he stared toward an unexpected sound— footsteps, which seemed to come, not up from the first

floor where Josephine should be arriving, but from some-where far down the poorly lit second-floor hallway.

He saw someone then, an indefinite shape moving swiftly toward him through the shadows. It was a woman, all right, but not, he soon realized, long-legged, broad-shouldered Cousin Josephine. The person gliding toward him was slim and slight, and her hair, instead of being knotted sensibly behind her head, floated out around her face in a cloudy gray halo.

Harleigh swallowed hard once, and then once more, before he realized that the strange apparition was only — Cousin Sheila. No, not *Cousin* Sheila, at least not to most of the Weatherbys, because of their doubts about the way in which she had descended. Just plain old Sad Sheila, the weird woman whose weeping and wailing had become a kind of family joke. Harleigh was disappointed. He didn't even bother to slide down off the chest, but when she was very near he did stifle a yawn and say hello.

Sheila — who until that moment apparently hadn't noticed his presence on the Chinese chest — came to an abrupt stop, her hands flying up to stifle a frightened gasp. There didn't seem to be any tears on her cheeks, and he hadn't heard any weeping or wailing, but there was some-thing about the slope of her eyebrows that suddenly reminded Harleigh of what Allegra had said about Sheila's

sad story. How Allegra had seemed so surprised and disappointed when he said he'd never even tried to find out more about it.

Uncrossing his legs, Harleigh slid down off the chest and said, "Hello. You're Sheila, aren't you? I'm Harleigh."

Sheila's expression changed from shock, to surprise, to a quiver that was almost a smile. "Yes," she said. "I know who you are, but I don't think we've really been introduced. You're the fourth Harleigh, aren't you?" She put out her hand. "I'm glad to meet you, Harleigh the Fourth."

"Me too." Harleigh nodded. He looked up briefly into her sad eyes, down at his shoes, and then up again. "I'm waiting for someone else right now," he said. "But I'd like to talk to you someday. Okay?"

"Yes." Sheila's sorrow-slanted eyes again widened in surprise. "Yes," she said, definitely smiling now. "I'd like that too." Then she drifted on, stopping once to look back, before she disappeared down the stairs. Watching her go, Harleigh remembered Aunt Adelaide's comment about how Sad Sheila's face resembled the mask of tragedy that you sometimes saw on the walls of auditoriums. Which wasn't quite true. At least not all the time.

Seated again on the chest, Harleigh went on waiting for Cousin Josephine, and while he waited he wondered if he would see Sheila again soon, and if he did, if he might

be able to hear her sad story. No particular reason, except that having actually met her seemed to have aroused his curiosity.

A few minutes later Cousin Josephine came tromping up the stairs. She was moving fast as she passed Harleigh without seeming to notice him. Jumping down off the chest, he was almost running before he caught up with her.

"Cousin Josephine," he called. "Wait a minute. Wait for me." She stopped then, looked back, and continued down the hall. It wasn't until Harleigh passed her and turned to face her that her pace slowed.

She frowned down at him as she demanded, "What do *you* want, Harleigh?"

He was puzzled. Cousin Josephine had never been a particular friend, but he couldn't remember her being quite so obviously unfriendly. "I just want to ask you a question," he said quickly as she tried to get around him. "Just one question."

Finally she stopped, still eyeing him suspiciously. "And what question would that be?"

"It's about something Aunt Adelaide told me. She said that you thought I was in her room when she wasn't there, and I did something I shouldn't have. She didn't say exactly what."

Josephine's head was cocked and her eyes were hard as

she said, "And you're saying you weren't? You didn't come into her room when no one was there and get into things like the crystal cabinet? And paw through some of the drawers in her desk?" Cousin Josephine shook her head and sighed. "None of this would have happened if only she'd listened to me when I urged her to get that lock repaired, but no, she was so sure that no Weatherby would think of intruding on her privacy." Her eyes narrowed angrily as she stared down at Harleigh. "And especially not a child she had such high hopes for."

"But it wasn't me." Harleigh insisted. Harleigh paused, gulped, and then went on. "But I think I know who might have done it."

Josephine's stare became even more intense and suspicious. "What do you mean, you think you know?"

"Well, I was just wondering if whoever it was might have been doing something up on the stage?"

"On the stage?" Cousin Josephine's stare was both amazed and disbelieving.

"You know. The stage in the recital hall. In Aunt Adelaide's room. I just wondered because—because somebody thought . . . I mean *I* thought I heard someone there. Up there on the stage."

"I see. And where, may I ask, were you when you heard this mysterious someone?"

"I was just—just walking by. Out in the hall. That's when I thought I heard something."

Judging by the expression on Cousin Josephine's face, Harleigh knew he was only making things worse—telling a story he only halfway believed himself, and one that she obviously didn't believe at all. Shrugging, he gave up and walked away. She didn't follow him or call for him to come back, but when he glanced over his shoulder she was still standing there, staring after him. He hurried on.

This time he didn't stop until he was halfway up the iron stairs that circled the tower wall, but his steps kept getting slower and slower until he finally decided to sit down and think—or at least try to. Halfway up the winding staircase, he sat staring down, way down, into the dimly lit, circular space and tried to organize his thoughts.

He hadn't believed it when Allegra said she heard a metal detector on the stage of the recital hall. But now it seemed that someone had been there, or at least somewhere in the recital hall, and whoever it was apparently had done some things they shouldn't have. Some things Aunt Adelaide and Cousin Josephine were now trying to blame on Harleigh. But he knew he wasn't guilty, so somebody else had to be.

And that brought up a new subject. The subject of whether or not Allegra really had seen Junior on a moonlit night swinging a metal detector over the dead lawn. And if

she had, whether it had made a noise that she might have recognized if she ever heard it again.

Which brought up a new question that Harleigh knew he wasn't ready to deal with. Not yet. Maybe not ever. A question that nobody except Junior himself could answer. So, Harleigh reasoned, it would seem that the next step was to march right up to Junior Weatherby and . . . Harleigh began to picture the scene. Pictured himself, not-even-normal-sized Harleigh Four, walking up to enormous old Junior and demanding to know whether he owned a metal detector. And if he did, whether or not he'd had it with him while he was making a secret visit to Aunt Adelaide's recital hall bedroom. And while he was at it, he might as well go on and demand to know exactly what he, Junior, thought he was looking for. Just imagining how that bit of detective work might turn out made the hair on the back of Harleigh's neck stand straight up.

So maybe not. At least not yet. But meanwhile, there was another important bit of information that would be a lot easier—and safer—to get. Information that probably could be provided by safe old Uncle Edgar instead of the scary individual who called himself Junior Weatherby.

Yes. Uncle Edgar, who knew so much about so many things, might be useful. But that would have to be tomorrow, when he went to the library for his lesson. Harleigh got to his feet and trudged on up to his room.

# Chapter Fifteen

By the next morning Harleigh had decided on the questions he needed to ask Uncle Edgar, as well as how he might go about asking them without giving away too much about what he was really trying to find out. The first question would be about sonar, or perhaps radar — just to make it sound as if he were looking for general information about machines that searched for things, and perhaps made a noise while they were doing it. But then he would get around to metal detectors and maybe find out what they looked like, and what kind of searches they were usually used for. *And* — this was especially important — if they made a noise while they were doing it.

Sure enough, Uncle Edgar had lots of useful information.

He even drew a picture of a long pole with some handles at one end and a large circular scanner at the other. And when Harleigh asked the important question, about what they sounded like, he said, "Well, I believe some of the newer ones have a small console on which symbols indicate whether anything made of metal has been located. But some of them still have audible indicators."

"What kind of indicators?" Harleigh asked.

Uncle Edgar smiled. "Audible. Something that you hear."

Something that you *hear*! That was it—exactly what Harleigh had been looking for. Or maybe what he hadn't been looking for, if he wanted to go on believing that Allegra had been lying when she said she'd heard a metal detector on the recital hall's stage.

Harleigh had a hard time keeping his mind on the rest of what Uncle Edgar wanted him to learn that morning, such as the relationship between diameters and circumferences and the dates of several ancient civilizations.

Finally Uncle Edgar said, "Well, it seems our recently improved attention span is taking the day off." His big, floppy grin spread across his face. "What's on your mind, boy?"

In the past, when Uncle Edgar said something of that sort, Harleigh might have let him have it with a quick comeback about how some teachers made their lessons interesting, while some others just didn't have the knack.

But today it somehow didn't seem worth the effort.

So all he said was that he had been working on a different sort of problem—a personal one. And when Uncle Edgar said he'd be glad to help if it were possible, Harleigh surprised himself by saying, "Yeah, well, I wish it was." The surprising part was—it was true.

It was almost noon before Uncle Edgar gave up on Harleigh, and even then he might not have, except that he was anxious to get to the special feast that Matilda was preparing.

"Special feast?" Harleigh asked. "What is she doing that for?"

Uncle Edgar stared at him. "He didn't tell you?" he said. "No one told you?" Uncle Edgar seemed very surprised.

"Your father didn't tell you?" he went on asking, and when Harleigh said no, Uncle Edgar shook his head and made the harrumphing noise that usually meant he was displeased about something. "You didn't know that your father was leaving for Australia today?"

"Today?" Harleigh was surprised. "But he just got here yesterday."

Uncle Edgar harrumphed again and sighed before he said, "That's true, but, it seems there's some remarkable new building going up down that way that he feels he needs to look over and write an article about. So actually the visit

here was only a stopover on his way. So now he's off to Down Under, and it seems our Matilda is preparing a feast in honor of his brief visit. So come on, boy. Let's give our heads a rest and go fill our stomachs."

Uncle Edgar was right, as usual. Not only about Matilda preparing a special meal with ham and sweet potatoes, which was Harleigh the Third's favorite menu, but also about the fact that Harleigh J. Weatherby the Third was about to leave again. But something else that soon became obvious was that Uncle Edgar was in a bad mood, glowering and grumping, in between mouthfuls of ham, at everything and everybody, especially at Harleigh the Third. Saying sarcastic things like how he supposed the rest of the family ought to feel fortunate to have another generous visit from Aunt Adelaide's heir apparent. "Aren't we fortunate," he said, "to have him with us for two whole days, and only six months from his last royal appearance?"

After a while Harleigh Four's father said, "Well, Edgar, I must say, you don't seem to be in a very pleasant frame of mind."

Then Uncle Edgar held his hand up in front of his mouth and lowered his voice. But not so much that it kept Harleigh Four from figuring out that what Uncle Edgar was upset about was that no one had told "the boy" his father was about to leave.

The two of them went on whispering for a while, with Harleigh the Third making excuses that Harleigh Four didn't bother to try to overhear. He was used to that sort of thing. And besides, he had more important problems to worry about.

When the meal was over, Harleigh Four's father did his usual hand-on-the-shoulder thing and said, "Good-bye, son," and that was the end of it. But at least there was nothing at all said about whether or not his son had been snooping around in Aunt Adelaide's room. So that was all right. Harleigh Four wasn't going to waste any time wondering whether his father hadn't been told about Josephine's suspicions or if he had heard and just didn't care. Harleigh Four had other things on his mind, such as how he was going to go about finding out whether Junior Weatherby owned a metal detector.

That same day, an hour or so after the taxi arrived to take his father to the airport, Harleigh Four's investigation to discover the truth about Cousin Junior and the metal detector was once more underway. Not moving very rapidly, perhaps, but definitely underway.

One reason he was making such slow progress was simply because there really was quite a long distance to cover. Harleigh had been to where Junior lived in the south ell of the west wing a couple of times before, but

not recently, and he wasn't too sure of the exact location. The other reason he wasn't moving very quickly was that he was finding it necessary to stop now and then to think and plan ahead. To make plans such as—what exactly he was going to do once he arrived at his destination.

It wasn't likely, he had decided, that Junior would be at home in the early afternoon of a weekday in summer. Which was actually what he was counting on. But on the other hand, it was equally unlikely that the doors to his rooms would be unlocked or that his metal detector—if he had one—would be right out in plain view of anyone who happened to pass by.

So what was Harleigh Four planning to do? Good question. Perhaps, if he was lucky, someone else would happen along—one of the other southern ell residents. Besides Sad Sheila there were, for instance, several more or less retired people who lived in the general area. There was A. J., the would-be lawyer; an old married couple called the Farleys; plus the Galworthy Girls, a pair of slightly identical twin sisters. All of whom were Weatherby descendants, of course, but only third or fourth cousins several times removed. But any one of them might have noticed Junior coming or going in possession of a long, strange-looking mechanism with a metal loop at the end.

That was beginning to sound like a plan. He would look

for the twins or the Farleys or some other relatively nearby relative who would surely have noticed Junior's metal detector if he had one. Somewhat comforted by having come up with a plan of action, Harleigh began to walk a little faster, but not so fast that he didn't take careful note of his surroundings.

The second ell off the west hall, which must once have been the living quarters of servants, or else rooms for very unimportant guests, was quite different from the grand corridors in the central building. Harleigh had forgotten how narrow the halls became as you turned into the ell, and also how little light came in through the widely spaced windows. He'd also forgotten, if he'd ever noticed it before, the strangely depressing smell.

The smell was—different. Not exactly dirty. Closer to heavy, perhaps, as if the air was dusty with memories of so many long, empty years. Stopping to sniff uneasily, Harleigh couldn't help remembering how Allegra had carried on about feeling, even hearing, the stories of early Weatherbys. He also remembered how ridiculous he'd thought the whole idea was, and how he'd certainly told her so. But now, breathing in the strangely time-heavy air, he wasn't so sure.

Shaking his head, Harleigh squared his shoulders and marched on down the long, dim hall, passing many doors that led into long-forgotten rooms, where who knows how

many people had spent their unimportant lives. He was still
deep in thought when another turn, and a short flight of
stairs, brought him to where he began to be aware that he
was once more where people were still actually living.
Where the light was a little brighter and there were sounds
of sorts, water running, and the faint shuffle of footsteps.
He had paused to listen more carefully when, only a few feet
away, a door slammed open and someone came out into the
dim light of the hallway. A huge, bushy-haired person with
a long hooked nose and narrow, twitchy eyes: Junior
Weatherby himself.

# Chapter Sixteen

**M**omentarily overcome by confusion, Harleigh froze. He had prepared himself for a meeting with the ancient Farleys or some other distant relation, but not Junior in person. A Junior who should have been surprised to find Harleigh J. Weatherby the Fourth practically on his doorstep, but if he was, it wasn't all that noticeable. What was noticeable was something a lot more unpleasant than surprise. When Junior said, "Well, look who we have way out here all by himself, *little* old Harleigh the Fourth," what it sounded as well as felt like was—a threat. Not only a threat, but an insult as well.

Harleigh Four was jolted for a moment before he took a deep breath and reminded himself that Weatherbys, real,

direct-descendant Weatherbys, *little* or not, didn't like to be threatened. He squared his shoulders, lifted his chin, and said, "Hello, Junior. I've come to ask about your metal detector. What I want to know is . . ."

That was as far as he got. At that point Junior's big right hand shot out and grabbed Harleigh's shoulder and shook him hard. So hard that the rest of what he'd planned to say was shaken right out of his mind, or at least off his tongue.

"What's that?" Junior was snarling. "What you talking about, kid? What makes you think I got a metal detector?"

Harleigh tried to answer. Opening his mouth, he tried to say—something. Anything at all, but nothing came out. Nothing. Not even "Stop that!" or "Turn me loose!" But then, while he was still being shaken and still desperately trying to say something, he was vaguely aware that, behind Junior's back, someone or something was approaching. And then, just at that life-or-death moment, a shrill voice said, "Stop that! What do you think you're doing?"

At the shockingly unexpected sound of that voice, the grip on Harleigh's shoulder loosened for just a moment. But that brief moment was all it took. A quick step backward, a twisting turn, and Harleigh was free and running back the way he had come.

He ran fast and hard, imagining Junior running after him, reaching out to grab him again, but as he reached the short

flight of stairs leading into the west hall, he began to realize he was alone. No one was running behind him. Or not, at least, close behind him. He slowed his pace enough to be able to glance back over his shoulder. No one was there. He staggered to a stop, breathing hard and straining to hear whether or not he was being followed. Silence. A silence that lasted only a second and then, just as he feared, there it was. No doubt about it. The sound of approaching footsteps.

As Harleigh turned to run, his eyes happened to fall on a door. A door, almost within arm's reach, which was probably locked, but just maybe . . . The door opened, and Harleigh slipped through and closed it behind him.

It was dark. Unable to see and fearing that any movement, any stumble or bump, would be heard by his pursuer, Harleigh stayed where he was. Leaning against the door, he listened as the sound of footsteps came nearer.

Nearer, but not much louder, and certainly not running. And then there was something else. Another sound. A voice. A familiar, breathy voice saying, "Harleigh. Harleigh, where are you?"

It was then that Harleigh realized who it was that he had seen approaching while he was being shaken by Junior. He hadn't recognized the voice that demanded that Junior stop what he was doing. But there had been just the quickest glimpse of a thin figure with a gray cloud of hair. And now,

remembering the voice, Harleigh suddenly knew. Just to be absolutely sure, he waited until she called once more before he cautiously opened the door.

It was Sheila all right, thin and wispy, with eyebrows that tilted down toward sorrow, but when she saw Harleigh, there was that quick, surprising smile.

After peering carefully around and behind her, Harleigh whispered, "Where is he? Where did Junior go?"

"He's gone," she said. "After you ran away, he went back into his room and slammed the door. I don't think he's following us."

As Harleigh was slowly and cautiously leaving his hideout, Sheila said, "Well, hello again, Harleigh Four. Were you coming to see me?"

"Coming to see you?" It was a question, but Sheila seemed to take it for an answer.

"I thought that might have been what brought you all the way out here. I'm so pleased. But then to have that dreadful man attack you that way. Why would he do such a thing?"

Still worried that Junior might appear at any moment, Harleigh only shook his head, mumbled, "I'd better go," and hurried on down the dark, narrow passageway. But Sheila came too, her gliding stride keeping up with Harleigh's nervous trot. They hadn't gone far when she once again started to ask about Junior. "I can't understand

it," she said. "Did you do anything at all to provoke him?"

Harleigh stopped long enough to check behind them again. Still no sign of Junior. "I only asked him if he has a metal detector," he said. A new idea occurred to him. "Maybe you know. Do you know if he has one?"

"A metal detector?" Sheila looked and sounded puzzled. "I don't know. What would it look like?"

But even after Harleigh described the long pole with handles on one end and a flat circular device on the other, she still shook her head. She hadn't seen Junior Weatherby with a metal detector. "But why would that make him so angry?" she wanted to know.

Lowering his voice, Harleigh said, "I don't know. Except that someone's been using one in . . ." He paused and then went on, "around Weatherby House. I know because we — because I heard it. And whoever it was, he was where he shouldn't have been, and doing something he shouldn't have been doing."

"Oh, I see," Sheila said. "Yes, I do see."

It wasn't until they were back in the familiar grandeur of the mansion proper that their pace slowed. In the central hall they came to a stop near where an elaborately carved mahogany bench sat beneath a large painting of a young woman in a high-necked dress holding a small dog in her lap.

"Now," Sheila's voice was once again so soft that Harleigh had to strain to hear, "you said you wanted to talk to me."

Harleigh blinked, wondering for just a moment what she was talking about before he remembered he'd said exactly that. He also remembered what he'd wanted to ask about and why. It all came from what Allegra said about Sheila's "sad story." Something about the way she'd said it, with a deep sigh and a slow shake of her head, made him curious.

Not that he was often curious about other people's stories, sad or otherwise. But now he found himself wanting to know not only how Allegra knew about it, but also about the story itself. Sitting down on the mahogany bench, he waited only long enough for Sheila to sit beside him before he began, "Tell me . . . that is, I'd like to know — to know . . ." He stammered to a stop and then came up with, "Why did you come to live in Weatherby House, and where did you live before that?"

It turned out to be a long story. A long story about the same kinds of bad things that happen to a lot of people. Things about deaths and desertions, and unwelcoming relatives, and how, when she was working as a secretary, a disloyal friend told lies about her that made her lose her job. But for some reason, maybe just really listening in person to

the storyteller, it seemed more . . . more what? More real and alive, maybe. So alive that listening to parts of it made Harleigh's eyes burn and his throat tighten.

He didn't like the feeling, but when the telling was over and Sheila thanked him for being such a good listener and said she felt better, he did too. And then, remembering the disapproving way Allegra looked at him when he told her he didn't know what Sheila was sad about, he liked thinking how much he'd have to say if the subject ever came up again.

It wasn't until Sheila left and Harleigh was on his way up to the tower that he remembered that he'd decided there wasn't going to be a next time. That he was through with Allegra, once and for all.

No more Allegra, except . . . except that some things had changed since he made that decision. Of course, some things were still the same. He was still angry about how she'd forced her way into the House and then run away to explore on her own. But what *had* changed was the fact that she probably had not been lying when she said she'd heard a metal detector on the stage in Aunt Adelaide's recital hall bedroom. So maybe he'd change his mind enough to see her one more time, just long enough to tell her Shelia's story, as well as all about what Junior had done to him, and what Junior might have done to him if Shelia hadn't happened to come along. A couple of events that

ought to really impress a person who was so interested in other people's stories.

While he was still trudging up the steep circular stairs, Harleigh was beginning to plan his next visit to the black walnut tree and Allegra.

# Chapter Seventeen

It was late that same night, or maybe very early the next morning, when Harleigh Four came up from the depths of a sound sleep with a vague feeling that he'd heard something. Someone on the stairs, perhaps? A rattling noise on the iron stairway that led to his tower bedroom? Sitting straight up, he stared wide-eyed toward the door while he listened breathlessly for the sound to be repeated.

Time passed. A faint hint of moonlight, seeping in through the Aerie's many windows, was not enough to dispel the threatening shadows that seemed to ooze around the base of the circular wall, clumping together here and there to form slightly sinister shapes. Many long, anxious

minutes crept by while Harleigh watched and listened and waited for something terrible to happen.

But nothing did. Whatever or whoever it was apparently had decided not to open the door—must not even have tried to, since there was no lock, and whoever it was could have walked right in. It was a troubling thought, and long before daylight arrived Harleigh had decided he had to do something about it.

It would have to be done very secretively. Aunt Adelaide would never agree to let him put a dead bolt lock on the door to the Aerie, and even if Uncle Edgar did, chances were that he would not be able to climb the tower staircase to help install it. The only other possibility, Harleigh decided, was Ralph the gardener, and that wasn't a very good one. Ralph was old and grouchy, and probably couldn't handle the stairs any better than Uncle Edgar. So it was without much hope that Harleigh went to the solarium that morning as soon as he'd finished his Friday lessons.

Sure enough, when Harleigh finally located Old Ralph in the orchid room at the far end of the solarium, it seemed obvious that he was, as usual, in a grouchy mood. Looking up from where he was bending stiffly over a watering can, his frown was almost hidden by a curtain of frowsy white hair, but his thin lips were set in an angry growl. When Harleigh said, "Good morning, Ral"—What was his last

name? Oh, yes, Olsen—"Good morning, Mr. Olsen," the old man straightened up slowly with one hand on his back.

"Here. Let me help you with that," Harleigh said, surprising himself almost as much as it seemed to surprise Mr. Ralph Olsen. The end of the encounter was surprising, too. By the time Harleigh had watered all the orchids and even managed to catch a large insect for the Venus flytrap, he'd finished explaining that he was interested in owning a dead bolt lock. So then Mr. Olsen found one in his storeroom, taught Harleigh how to install it, and didn't even ask what door it was for.

Harleigh was about to leave with the lock and a paper bag full of the necessary tools, when the old man pushed the hair out of his eyes, stared at Harleigh, and said, "Yer growin'. Ain't you?" Of course Harleigh knew better, but it seemed like Old Ralph meant well, so he just smiled and thanked him and said good-bye.

That was on Friday, and Harleigh slept better that night and the two that followed. Once or twice he did hear, or dreamed he'd heard, someone on the stairs. A metallic clatter that started far away and then came closer and got louder. And one time there'd even been a faint clicking sound that seemed to come from the door. As if someone might have tried and failed, because of the dead bolt, to open it. It worried him some, even though he wasn't entirely sure it hadn't

all been part of a dream. But it would have worried him a lot more if he hadn't known that the Aerie's door was firmly dead-bolted shut.

He was still, however, doing a certain amount of lying awake, which gave him lots of time to think about the fact that he now knew that Junior probably *had* been using a metal detector in Aunt Adelaide's bedroom. And there was the even more disturbing fact that Junior might have guessed that he knew. The longer he thought about the situation, the more he wanted to tell someone the whole story.

Someone, but definitely not Aunt Adelaide and Cousin Josephine. He wasn't sure why, except that he had no way to prove any of it, and he knew they would think it was just a wild story he'd made up to cover the fact that he himself had been prowling around and doing some kind of damage in Aunt Adelaide's private living quarters.

But then there was Uncle Edgar. Harleigh briefly considered telling him the whole story, except that the telling would have to include the metal detector, and that would involve mentioning—Allegra. And not just a brief mention. After all, if Allegra hadn't seen Junior using the metal detector on that moonlit night, and then if she hadn't heard him using it on the recital hall stage, there was no way Harleigh would have known anything about it.

But Allegra was the one subject Harleigh couldn't

imagine mentioning to anyone. Certainly nothing concerning her dangerous visit to Weatherby House, and not even who she was. Especially not who she was. He didn't know why that was true, except that any question about Allegra's identity was one he really didn't know how to answer.

And besides, before Uncle Edgar would do anything he'd probably feel he had to tell Aunt Adelaide the whole story, which she probably wouldn't believe coming from him, any more than she would if it came directly from Harleigh.

Of course, there was one person who did know some of the truth about Junior, and that was Sheila. At least she knew about how he had attacked Harleigh just because he asked about a metal detector. But what Sheila knew or didn't know unfortunately didn't make any difference one way or another, since none of the other Weatherbys would pay any attention to anything poor Sad Sheila had to say.

So it was no wonder he was anxious to see Allegra again. Not that she could do anything to help the situation, but at least she would be someone to talk to.

# Chapter Eighteen

But when Monday morning finally came, Allegra was late as usual. Sitting there in the tree house, waiting for her as the minutes dragged by, would have put Harleigh in a really bad mood, except for the fact that he had finally managed to climb up the way Allegra always did, with only one metal rod in place. And that accomplishment improved his state of mind so much that when he heard a faint noise and turned just in time to see Allegra's head appearing over the edge of the tree house floor, he felt quite calm. At least a lot calmer than he'd expected to be.

"Harleigh!" Allegra squealed delightedly the moment she saw him. "Where have you been? I've been so worried about you. Are you all right?"

"All right?" Harleigh said. "Of course I'm all right. I just didn't come because I was angry. At you."

"Angry at me?" Allegra looked amazed. "Why were you angry at me?"

"You mean you don't have any idea?" Harleigh snorted. "Don't you remember pushing your way into the house and then running away when I was trying to get you out, and—"

"Oh, that." Allegra shrugged and smiled. "But everything turned out all right, didn't it?"

"Just barely. We were just very lucky that door in the west wing wasn't locked."

"Oh? 'Cause it's usually locked?" She sounded doubtful.

"Of course," Harleigh said. "It's one of the rules."

"Oh," Allegra said again. "I thought maybe it usually wasn't." She nodded thoughtfully. "Some doors are usually unlocked, and . . ." Her smile was knowing, almost teasing. "And some doors are locked that didn't used to be."

Harleigh was about to ask her what she meant by that, but it was right then that she asked a different question.

"And what about the metal detector?" she suddenly said.

"Well, that was the other thing I wanted to talk about," Harleigh said. He went on to tell her how he found out about the noise that metal detectors make, and how he now knew that someone had been in the recital hall and had done some damage. And that he, Harleigh, was being accused of

having done it. "I didn't believe it when you said you heard it up there on the stage, but now I do."

He waited for her to say, "I told you so." But all she did was to cock her head to one side, the way she did when she was thinking, before she said, "What do you think he was looking for?"

Harleigh shook his head. "Same as before, I guess. The Weatherby buried treasure. But the worst part of it is, that he must have guessed that I know what he's been doing. Anyway, he's really angry at me for some reason. Wait till I tell you what happened."

So he did. The whole story about how he went all the way to the servants' ell at the end of the west wing, and how he met Junior and asked him about his metal detector, and how Junior just about shook him to death, and probably would have if Sheila hadn't come along.

Allegra's reaction to the story—wide eyes and several sharp gasps—was about what Harleigh expected, but what she said next wasn't. Instead of some ideas about what ought to be done about Junior, she only stared into space for a long time without saying anything. And when she finally did, it was only, "And how about Sheila? Is she all right?"

Some seconds ticked by while Harleigh considered some remarks such as, "Sheila? She wasn't the one who got attacked, remember? I was the one Junior almost shook to

death." But he finally settled for, "She's all right." But then he remembered how he had planned to tell Allegra that he now knew everything about Sheila's sad story, so he added, "That is, she's fine except for the fact that she's had this terrible life. I mean, you wouldn't believe all the horrible things that have happened to her. She told me all about it."

Allegra nodded eagerly. "She did? Tell me," she said.

So he did. All about the tragic deaths and treacherous friends and all the rest of it. Allegra listened, wide-eyed, hardly seeming to breathe, and when Harleigh finished, she said, "Yes. I thought it must have been something like that. No wonder she cries a lot." Then she sighed again and shook her head before saying, "So you think Junior was looking for the treasure when we heard him in Aunt Adelaide's room?"

It took a moment for Harleigh to switch back over from Sheila's troubles, but when he did, he said, "I guess so. Just like when you saw him that night out on the lawn."

"Hmm." Allegra stared into space a moment before she said, "I wonder what kind of treasure. Something made of metal, I guess."

Harleigh snorted. "Well, what else do you look for with a metal detector? But I guess it could be jewels or money in a metal box. In a metal box under the floor of the stage. The stage is up about this high." Harleigh held up his hand

to indicate the height of the stage. "A whole lot of treasure could be hidden in between the two floors."

"Yes." Allegra's eyes were alight. "I think you're right."

Harleigh thought he was right too. He could almost see it. A large open area under the stage floor where stacks of metal boxes overflowed with the famous Weatherby buried treasure. The very thought of it was like a magnet pulling him back toward the house. Getting to his feet, he said, "I'd better go now."

"Now?" Allegra looked shocked and surprised. "Aren't we going to work in the maze today? At least just a little. I think we only have a little more to do."

"A little more to do before what?" Harleigh asked.

"Before we get to the end. I think we're almost there." She rolled her eyes thoughtfully. "I think it's important to find the exit very soon."

"Why is that? Why does it matter when we do it?"

She shook her head slowly. "I'm not sure why. But I just think it does."

Harleigh finally agreed, but even after they got to the maze and started to work, they didn't get much done. Every few feet one of them would stop shearing and clipping to share another idea about what the treasure might be, and whether it really was under the floor of the stage, or whether Junior had already managed to steal it.

"Wouldn't your aunt and Josephine know if it was already gone?" Allegra wanted to know.

Harleigh stopped briefly in midclip. "No, I don't think so," he decided. "There's a curtain between the stage and the rest of the room, and no one goes up there anymore. They might not even notice. But Junior might not have had a chance to do it yet.

"The thing is," he went on to explain, "I think he must have just found out where the treasure is when we heard his metal detector, but right then Aunt Adelaide had only gone to the kitchen or something, so he didn't have very long. He'd probably have to tear a hole in the stage floor to get the treasure out, and that would be noisy and take a lot more time. I guess he could have done it later while Aunt Adelaide and Josephine were somewhere else in the house, but I think it's more likely he's waiting to do it when they go to town again."

"Don't you think he might be in a hurry because you know about his metal detector?" Allegra said.

Harleigh had to think about that for a minute before he said, "Maybe not. All he knows is that I think he has one, like maybe I heard someone talking about it. He probably doesn't know we heard it on the recital hall's stage."

"When will Aunt Adelaide go to town again?" Allegra asked.

"Usually they go on Mondays," Harleigh told her. "But yesterday at breakfast I heard Aunt Adelaide telling Matilda she'd be going on Wednesday this week because she has a dentist appointment. So I guess that means . . ."

"Day after tomorrow," Allegra said. "But how would Junior know when she goes away?"

That was another question Harleigh had to think over. "He could find out pretty easily," he said at last. "He could ask Ralph. Ralph always drives the car. Or else he could just watch for her to leave. That wouldn't be hard for him to do. Ralph has to drive around to the front entrance, and then he and Josephine load Aunt Adelaide and her wheelchair into the car. And then they have to go all the way around the circular drive on their way to the gate."

"Yes," Allegra said. "I think he's probably waiting for her to go to town. And then he'll have time to tear up the floor and get the treasure out. Unless we can do something to stop him." And then, speaking in a thoughtful tone of voice, she asked, "What will we do to stop him?"

Harleigh snipped off a few more twigs before he suddenly whirled around to face Allegra. "What do you mean, 'we'? You're not going to be there."

He stared at Allegra and she stared back, her gray eyes wide open and innocent. Or at least, wide open. At last she turned away, and reaching way up over her head, she clipped

off two or three branches before saying, "Yes, I know. I meant what will *you* do? I won't be there." She clipped some more before she said, "What will *you* do to stop him?"

Harleigh shook his head slowly, thought some more, and shook it again.

"What?" Allegra pressed him.

"I guess I could warn Aunt Adelaide about what he's planning, except . . ."

"Except?"

"Well, if she believed me enough to stay home to wait for Junior to come, he would see that the car hadn't gone out, so he wouldn't show up. I mean, he wouldn't be dumb enough to try it without checking to see if the car was gone. And then when he didn't show up, she'd be sure it was just a lie I made up to get him blamed for something she thinks I did. And I'm pretty sure she wouldn't call the police."

"Why not? Why wouldn't she tell the police?"

Harleigh grinned. "Because if it wasn't true and there was no treasure, she'd feel like a fool. And if it turned out to be true and there was a lot of money, she wouldn't want the government to know about it, because of things like taxes. Aunt Adelaide is against taxes."

"But wouldn't she at least check to see if there really was a treasure?"

"Well, she couldn't do it herself, could she? She can't

walk, and a wheelchair can't climb stairs. And I don't think she'd send Josephine up there to look. She wouldn't want Josephine to know."

Allegra looked surprised. Harleigh dodged another "Why not?" and went on to say, "I don't know, but I think it's because she doesn't trust anyone who's not a direct descendant. At least not where anything about money is concerned. I think she might tell my father, but he's in Australia."

"And there isn't anyone else you could tell? Someone who'd believe you?"

For a moment Harleigh considered Uncle Edgar again, and then dismissed that idea too. Uncle Edgar might believe him and might even want to help, but since Junior was a lot younger and stronger, there wasn't much he could do personally. And if all Uncle Edgar could do was tell someone like Aunt Adelaide, Harleigh could do that much by himself—if he had to.

It was still pretty early when Harleigh put down his shears and said he thought he had done enough maze work for the time being. But Allegra wanted to go on. "Just a little bit farther," she said. "Why not? Are you tired?"

"No," Harleigh said. "I'm not tired. I just have other things to do."

"To do, or to think about?" Allegra asked.

Harleigh shrugged. "To think about, I guess."

"Well, couldn't you think about them while we work? I think it's important for us to keep going a little longer."

That's what Allegra said, but when Harleigh asked her why, she only widened her eyes in that unfocused stare and said, "Because I think we're almost there."

Harleigh was skeptical. He checked the tangled thicket of yew branches blocking the path just ahead of them. They looked the same as always, maybe even a little thicker and pricklier.

Allegra was down on her knees, starting on some lower branches. Harleigh tapped her shoulder to get her attention. "How do you know we're almost there? You can't see the end, can you?"

She reached in farther and clipped again before she put down the shears and, lying on her stomach, peered into the small tunnel she'd started. "Almost," she said. "I can almost see it."

That was too much. As far as Harleigh was concerned, either you could see something or you couldn't. And at the moment, he had more important things to think about than word games. "Okay," he said. "Good for you. But I'm going."

"Wait," she said. "Wait, I'm coming." But he didn't wait, at least not really. He did pause now and then as he took the complicated route back to the entrance, skillfully

avoiding all the twists and turns that led to dead ends or else circled back to the main passageway, but if Allegra was following, she didn't catch up. Not in the maze, at least.

He had passed the black walnut tree's clearing and was about to start through the bamboo thicket, when suddenly she was there beside him. He stopped, and she did too.

"Where are *you* going?" he demanded.

"With you?" she asked. It was definitely a question, and one that she should have known the answer to.

"No, you're not," he said. "I'm going home."

"But about Junior—" she started to say, but he cut her off.

"I can take care of Junior." Right at that moment, with Allegra looking up into his face, he really believed what he was saying.

# Chapter Nineteen

By daylight the next morning Harleigh had decided on a plan of action. Actually, he'd considered a great number of them during the long, mind-numbing midnight hours, but by the time a foggy morning sun began to sift in through the Aerie's windows, he'd rejected most of them—including the one in which he would borrow the sword and shield from the entry hall's suit of armor, lie in wait for Junior just inside the recital hall door, and when Junior appeared he would leap out shouting. . . . Well, maybe not.

The one remaining plan had several advantages, the most important one being that it could be done right away, and until it was accomplished there was not much point in

trying to figure out what the next step would be. This plan
was simply to find out for sure whether Junior had already
stolen the treasure. Until then, he was finally able to con-
vince himself, there was no point in trying to decide what
should be done next.

As Harleigh, a bit groggy from lack of sleep, stumbled
out of bed and into his usual summer uniform (shorts and a
T-shirt), he reminded himself that he had to begin by finding out whether Aunt Adelaide and Josephine were planning to eat lunch in the kitchen or have it delivered to the
recital hall, as they often did. If they were planning to eat in
the kitchen, there would be plenty of time for him to get a
quick look at the stage floor. And he would only have to
stay long enough to discover whether it had already been
chopped or sawed open. It seemed simple enough.

Once in the kitchen, Harleigh's method of operation was
rather well planned. Instead of just asking Aunt Adelaide
and Josephine where they were eating, which might have
aroused their suspicions, he had decided to begin by talking
to Matilda. He would ask Matilda what they were having
for lunch, and then in the general discussion, Aunt Adelaide
might mention where she was intending to eat. So as soon
as he'd finished his toast and scrambled eggs, Harleigh went
over to where Matilda was doing something with a rolling
pin. He watched for a while as the rolling pin stretched and

flattened a large whitish blob before he said, "That looks . . ." He almost said "disgusting" before he caught himself. "That looks interesting. What is it?"

Matilda's blank face (a face that usually showed no expressions at all) changed to shocked surprise. Almost as if she didn't know Harleigh could talk. Or was it just surprise that he was talking to her?

Clearing her throat, she said in a rusty voice, "Crust. Crust for chicken pot pie."

"Oh yeah? That's going to be crust? For chicken pot pie?" Everyone, including Harleigh, liked Matilda's chicken pot pie. "And that's going to be the crust?" Harleigh watched a few more minutes, getting caught up in observing how the future crisp and tasty crust bulged unappetizingly out from under the rolling pin, first one way and then the other. So caught up that he momentarily forgot what he was doing. Suddenly remembering, he asked, "When is it going to be ready? I mean, will it be for *lunch* today?"

"Mmm," Matilda mumbled. "Lunch. Today."

"Chicken pot pie for lunch today," Harleigh announced loudly, glancing at Aunt Adelaide, hoping she'd say where she'd have hers. And then, just as he was beginning to wonder if she'd heard, she spoke to Matilda.

"When exactly?" Aunt Adelaide asked. "I do like my pastries to be right out of the oven. Should we be here at

twelve or twelve thirty, Matilda?" Then when Matilda said twelve, Aunt Adelaide said, "Good. We'll be here exactly at twelve."

So then he knew. Aunt Adelaide and Josephine would be in the kitchen at twelve sharp. And at 12:05 he, Harleigh the Fourth, would be making a quick inspection of the recital hall's stage.

Harleigh left for the library, determined to finish his Tuesday lessons in record time so he wouldn't risk being late. But it was then that things stopped going as planned. Every lesson seemed to drag by, either because Uncle Edgar had worked hard at coming up with the sneakiest math problems and most complicated Latin phrases he could possibly find, or just possibly because it was harder than usual for Harleigh to keep his mind on his work. Time practically stood still while Harleigh tried to concentrate, first on geometry and then on Latin verbs, while checking his watch every few minutes to be sure it wasn't yet twelve o'clock.

At last Uncle Edgar closed his book and, in a concerned tone of voice, said, "What's on your mind, boy?"

Harleigh made an effort to look as if Uncle Edgar's question not only bored but also puzzled him, but without much success. His "What do you mean?" was too quick and too defensive.

As Uncle Edgar went on staring at him questioningly,

Harleigh couldn't keep his eyes from sliding away shiftily as he asked, "Can I go now?" And then, without waiting for an answer, he went.

Out in the entry hall, Harleigh stopped to glance once more at his watch and was surprised to find that he had some time to spare. Only eleven forty-five. Not really time enough to get clear up to the tower and back, but more than enough to pick a hideout somewhere along Aunt Adelaide and Josephine's route to the kitchen.

It needed to be a place close enough to hear them go by, but not so close that he might risk being seen. Darting across the hall, he ran halfway through the drawing room before he stopped to look for the best hiding place. After quickly trying and rejecting spots behind some window drapes (too far away) and behind a French provincial chair (too exposed), he finally settled for flat on the floor behind a bulgy velvet love seat. At five minutes until twelve Harleigh had barely gotten into position when he began to hear the squealing squeak of the wheelchair. Aunt Adelaide, on her way to make sure her chicken pot pie was right out of the oven.

As soon as the last whisper of wheelchair sound had died away into silence, Harleigh stood up and, running on tiptoe, headed for the recital hall. And only seconds later he was quietly pushing open one of the big double doors.

It all seemed to be going well until, just as the door came

to a stop, something bounced off Harleigh's shoulder and landed near his feet. A dime. It was only a dime, but where had it come from? His first thought was that someone had thrown it, but a quick glance around reassured him that there was no one there. He was alone in the huge room, and a small coin had appeared out of nowhere and was now lying at his feet.

Turning slowly in a circle, Harleigh once again surveyed the room. Could someone have thrown the dime and then ducked down behind a piece of furniture? Behind Aunt Adelaide's massive desk, or the curtains of her canopied bed? A quick trip around the room produced nothing at all. As he looked carefully behind antique furniture, ancient artifacts, and paintings of people in old-fashioned clothing, some of Allegra's weird ideas about "stories" flicked the edges of his consciousness. Long enough to make him wonder briefly if Weatherby House's "storytellers" were capable of throwing things.

But he had other things to think about and to do quickly. By making a strong effort he forced himself to forget, at least for the time being, the whole strange event. After all, it was only a dime, and he had to put his mind on what he had come to do: to find out whether there were any openings in the stage floor, and if so, whether it meant that the treasure had already been stolen.

concerned. Realistically thinking, he had to admit, rounding up even two or three distant descendants would probably be next to impossible.

Another not very promising possibility involved locating Ralph and getting him to provide another dead bolt lock to take the place of the broken one on the recital hall's doors. Then, tomorrow morning, as soon as Aunt Adelaide and Josephine left for town, Harleigh would rush to the recital hall and install the lock. The chief drawback of that scheme was the fact that dead bolts can be locked only when you are inside the room, which meant that although Junior would be locked out, Harleigh himself would be locked in.

He'd gotten only about that far in his review of possible strategies, when suddenly there was a loud, determined knock on his door.

Surprised and startled, Harleigh stared at the door for several seconds before he answered. During that time the visitor knocked again and then tried to open the door. But Harleigh, as always recently, had slid the dead bolt into place when he entered the room, so the door rattled loudly but stayed shut. But when he finally managed to call, "Who is it?" the answering voice was loud—and slightly familiar.

"Come on, kid. Open up," a rather hoarse, breathless voice said, and it did sound a little like Cousin Josephine's

Behind the curtains that closed off the stage it was quite dark, but Harleigh, thinking back to the one time he'd explored the stage, seemed to remember some electric lights. Feeling along the wall near the stairs that led down to the performers' door, his fingers encountered a panel of switches. He began to flick them on, or try to, but the first two produced no light at all. He was beginning to think that all the old bulbs had burned out when the third switch produced a faint glow. Not a great deal of light, but enough to see that, just as he remembered, the stage was empty except for two old pianos: a big grand and, against the back wall, an ancient upright. It was also easy to see that the varnished planks that made up the stage floor were smooth and unbroken. So the treasure had not yet been stolen.

Switching off the light, Harleigh parted the curtains, jumped down to the recital hall's floor, and dashed across the room and out into the hall, closing the door firmly behind him. He reached the kitchen only ten minutes after twelve o'clock. Not much later than his usual tardy appearances.

Aunt Adelaide and Josephine were still at the table, as was Uncle Edgar, when Harleigh sat down to a serving of Matilda's tasty chicken pot pie. Feeling quite pleased with himself, he nodded and smiled to the others, especially Matilda, and started to eat. He had accomplished what he had set out to do. He'd managed to find out that the

treasure was safe, and now all that remained was to . . .

That's when the letdown hit him. All he'd actually done was to prove that he now had to go ahead and take the next step. The hard one. The one in which he would keep Junior from stealing the Weatherby treasure tomorrow morning while Aunt Adelaide and Josephine were in town.

# Chapter Twenty

**B**ack in his room at the top of the tower, Harleigh sat down on his bed and set to work going over some of the schemes he'd considered and then discarded the night before. They all seemed pretty hopeless. One very slim possibility was that tomorrow morning, as soon as Aunt Adelaide and Cousin Josephine left, he would be able to round up all the descendants he could locate and get them to come with him to the recital hall. The point being that Junior would find having so many witnesses to his crime more or less discouraging.

The weak points of this particular plan included the fact that most Weatherby descendants were rather stubborn and suspicious people, particularly where Harleigh Four was

husband, Cousin Alden. But maybe not. Harleigh stayed where he was. But then the voice came again. "It's Alden, kid. Open the door. I have to talk to you."

Yes. It really was Cousin Alden. Sliding off his bed, Harleigh hurried to the door and slid open the bolt. Josephine's scrawny little husband staggered into the room, huffing and puffing.

Cousin Alden wasn't a big man. Not nearly as fat as Uncle Edgar, nor as old as Ralph, but since he spent most of his time sitting around writing unpublished books, he was not in very good shape. Puffing and wheezing, he said, "They sent me to get you. They're in the library, and they want to talk to you right away."

Harleigh didn't ask who "they" was. When you got sent for in Weatherby House, you knew who was doing the sending. But after a moment, he did say, "Why?"

Cousin Alden's shrug seemed to bring on another attack of wheezes, but in between huffs and puffs he managed to get out, "Don't know exactly, kid. But I don't think she's delighted. Guess I've never seen Adelaide the Great in a great mood, but this one is something else again. You better get a move on."

So Harleigh did. Leaving Cousin Alden to struggle down all the stairs by himself, Harleigh raced down as far as the third floor before he slowed enough to take his mind off his

flying feet and try to put it on what was about to happen.

What could Great-Aunt Adelaide be upset about? She couldn't possibly know that he'd been in her room. He hadn't touched anything except the doorknob and the light switches on the stage, and he definitely hadn't moved or broken anything. And nobody had seen him on his way there or going into the recital hall. He was sure of that. There just wasn't any way anybody could know.

There were only three people in the library when Harleigh entered, a long-faced Cousin Josephine, a ruefully smiling Uncle Edgar, and a scowling Aunt Adelaide, whose wheelchair was pulled up facing the scowling picture of her famous ancestor, Harleigh the First.

As Harleigh Four approached, Aunt Adelaide said, "Come here, young man. No, over there. Stand right there where we can all see you." As soon as Harleigh took the place she indicated, directly in front of the famous portrait, she went on, "So then, tell us. Why were you in my room again, young man?"

"In your room?" Harleigh swallowed and blinked hard, while silently asking himself, *How could she know? How could she possibly know?*

"That's what I said. And don't try to deny it." Aunt Adelaide was almost shouting. "We have proof, don't we, Josephine?"

"Yes, I'm afraid we do." Josephine got up from where she'd been sitting next to Uncle Edgar.

"Proof?" Harleigh's voice had gone high and quavery.

"Tell him," Aunt Adelaide said. Nodding at Uncle Edgar, she went on. "Tell both of them."

"Yes, I will," Josephine said, looking at Uncle Edgar. "Ever since the last time, when he rummaged through Aunt Adelaide's desk as well as the octagonal cabinet, and managed to break one of the most valuable crystal ornaments, we've been taking precautions. I once again urged Aunt Adelaide to get the lock on the doors repaired right away, but she felt it would be a shame to set modern locking mechanisms into that beautiful wood. So she decided that for the time being we would only set a trap every time we left the room. A trap that would let us know if anyone had entered while we were away."

"A trap?" Uncle Edgar, whose smile up until that moment had seemed to say that he wasn't taking any of this too seriously, looked astonished.

*The dime,* Harleigh thought suddenly. *Something about the dime.* Shocked and suddenly frightened, Harleigh stepped backward sharply, whacking his head against the portrait's gilded frame. It really hurt. He was rubbing the painful spot as he heard Uncle Edgar asking, "What kind of a trap are we talking about?"

Cousin Josephine nodded smugly. "Each time we went out, I would simply reach up"—standing on her toes and stretching one long arm upward, she demonstrated—"I would reach up and balance a small coin on top of each of the doors. And then, when—"

"Yes, yes. I get the picture," Uncle Edgar said. Turning to Harleigh, he asked, "And was it you? Are you the one who opened the recital hall doors this morning?"

Possible answers flitted through Harleigh's throbbing head. He shook it again to shake off the pain and tried to think. He could tell Aunt Adelaide it hadn't been him. That someone else must have opened the door. He could make it a believable story. He was about to start when his eyes met Uncle Edgar's steady, unbending gaze.

And suddenly Harleigh found himself saying, "Yes. I opened the door, and I went in, too, and I could tell you why but you wouldn't believe me." Then he turned his back on all of them and ran out of the room.

Back in the tower, Harleigh stretched out across his bed and let his mind spin. He went over all of it. Over how it had been Allegra who had told him about seeing Junior looking for something with a metal detector. And then how they, the two of them, had heard him looking for, and probably finding out, where the long-lost treasure must be. But now . . .

But now it was Harleigh, Harleigh alone, who was going to suffer the consequences. It was he, Harleigh J. Weatherby the Fourth, who would surely be sent away to Hardacre Military Academy, where kids were whipped and yelled at, and those who weren't big, and good at sports, were teased and tormented.

Burying his face in his arms, he pictured how it would be. Pictured it all too clearly. He could almost see and feel the clenched fists and hear the taunting voices saying some of the things that had been said to him at Riverbend Elementary School. "What is it with you, anyway, kid, are you a midget? You sure you belong in this room? Come on, kiddy. We'll show you the way back to the kindergarten." He was still hearing the voices when he fell asleep, and then went on hearing them in his dreams.

When he woke up it was almost dark. He had slept right through dinnertime. Not that it mattered. They probably would have sent him to bed without his supper anyway. He got up and went to one of the windows. This time the sight of the endless expanse of Weatherby House stretching away to the east and west failed to comfort or even interest him. But because there was nothing else to do he stayed there, staring out into the gathering darkness. Eventually he found himself thinking of Allegra's story about someone who had spent many hours staring out of

the same window. But now, instead of shrugging, Harleigh shuddered.

He went back to sit on his bed with his face buried in his hands. Life was unfair, his head still hurt where he'd bumped it, and he was, he suddenly realized, very hungry. After listening to his growling stomach for several minutes, he stood up and growled back. "Why not? I can't be in any more trouble than I'm in already," and headed for the kitchen.

# Chapter Twenty-one

When Harleigh decided on a quick visit to the kitchen, it was after eight o'clock and his hopes were not particularly high. Leftovers from any meal where Uncle Edgar had been present were not a safe bet. But there would surely be something in the refrigerator or the pantry, if only a couple of slices of bread. What he was not counting on, at that hour of the night, was seeing, or being seen by, anybody. Not even by Matilda, who by now surely would have gone off to wherever it was she lived, somewhere in the servants' quarters in one of the branches of the west wing.

But when Harleigh pushed open the heavy swinging door, there she was at the kitchen table, writing something

in a notebook. Harleigh stared at her in consternation, and she stared back for a long nervous-making interval before anyone twitched a muscle. Harleigh made the first move. Remembering their surprisingly friendly encounter over the pie crust, he ventured a smile and said, "Hi, Matilda. I don't suppose there's any of that chicken pot pie left. That was really great chicken pot pie."

Matilda got slowly to her feet, and for an awful moment Harleigh thought she was going to grab him and drag him out of the kitchen and maybe all the way down the west corridor to Aunt Adelaide. But then a smile slowly penciled in across her big, blank face. "You hungry, boy?" she said, and without waiting for an answer she put down her pen and notebook and headed for the refrigerator.

Before long Harleigh was sitting at the table and Matilda was sitting across from him as he bit into a large, juicy roast beef sandwich. Matilda seemed to have lost interest in writing lists or menus, or whatever she'd been doing, and had settled down to watching Harleigh eat, while now and then offering brief observations.

"Yes," she said at one point, nodding and smiling. "Real hungry." And a minute later, "Too bad to starve a growing boy, no matter what he done."

Harvey smiled and nodded while he chewed. "I'm glad

you think so," he managed to say, but what he was thinking was, *You're right about me not deserving starvation, but not*—his lips twisted in a rueful grin—*but not about the growing part of it.*

"So, they going to send you away?" Matilda asked.

Harleigh stopped smiling, as a chill ran down his back. "Is that what they said?"

She nodded. "That's what they were saying at dinner. She said they'd be sending you away to a soldierin' school."

Harleigh didn't have to ask who *she* was or what soldierin' school they were talking about. The bite he was chewing stuck in his throat and he had to swallow hard before he said, "Yeah, I was afraid of that."

There was another long silence before Matilda said, "You don't want to go." It wasn't a question, so he didn't have to try to answer, which was a good thing, because the way she'd said it made his eyes burn and another bite of sandwich refuse to go down.

While he turned his face away, blinking and trying to swallow, Matilda got up and came around the table and stood there behind him for a moment before she patted him on the head.

That was what did it. Afterward he couldn't imagine why, except that it had been a bad day and that pat on his sore head reminded him that he was hurting in more ways

than one. For some reason that was the last straw, and for a minute he really lost it.

It was embarrassing. He hadn't cried for years and years, no matter what happened, not even during and after all the useless operations. Matilda wrapped up the rest of the sandwich, and as he headed for the door, she handed it to him without saying anything more.

It wasn't until Harleigh was back in his bed in the tower, trying to find a comfortable position for his sore head, that he realized that he'd been missing an important fact. It hadn't occurred to him before, but he seemed to have made a lump halfway up the back of his head by backing into something that he used to be able to stand under with at least an inch to spare. Did that mean . . . ?

It was an interesting thought. Fascinating, really. What it seemed to mean was that, after he'd given up on hoping, the third operation had really made a difference. He really had started to grow.

Getting out of bed, Harleigh went to the one of the cupboards that had once held supplies for the famous Weatherby sunset parties and took out a pile of clothing. He put aside the shorts he always wore during the warm Weatherby summers and dug out a pair of corduroys he hadn't worn for three or four months. They were only a little tight around his waist, but the length . . . He couldn't believe it. The pants that had

rested on the tops of his shoes just six months ago now ended way above his ankles. He really had started to grow.

Back in bed, Harleigh stared wide-eyed into darkness, while his mind whirled in confusing circles. At one moment he was thinking that he couldn't have found out that he was growing, and growing fast, at a better moment. At a moment when he really needed something to improve his state of mind.

And then, a minute later, he almost wished it hadn't happened. Not that he wished he hadn't started to grow. He'd never wish that. But just that finding out right now had made it hard for him to concentrate on how miserable he felt and how angry he was at all of them. At Aunt Adelaide for threatening to send him away to that awful school, and at Josephine for gloating about their stupid trap. And at Uncle Edgar, too, for being on Harleigh's side and not having the nerve to say so. And even a little bit at Matilda for making him embarrass himself, by giving him a sandwich and a pat on the head.

It took him a very long time to get to sleep, but when he finally did he slept hard, waking up the next morning to a dark, gloomy sky and a confusing mixture of emotions — resentment and anger along with a certain amount of excitement about the definitely outgrown corduroy pants. For a while he just lay there, wondering exactly how much taller

he actually was and how long it would take him to catch up to normal twelve-year-old height, before he suddenly remembered that this was *Wednesday*. The Wednesday when Aunt Adelaide and Josephine would go to town and Junior Weatherby would probably try his hand at a very important robbery.

Wrenching his mind away from all of the rest of it, the good and the bad, Harleigh focused instead on the problem at hand. The huge problem of what, if anything, he could do to protect the Weatherby treasure.

# Chapter Twenty-two

It was a strange breakfast. Aunt Adelaide was at her grimmest, and Cousin Josephine was not far behind. Uncle Edgar looked even gloomier than usual, but not melancholy enough, it seemed, to spoil his appetite. Nobody, except maybe Matilda, so much as looked in Harleigh's direction when he came in. He took his place at the table without saying anything, and it wasn't until the meal was almost over that anyone said anything at all.

It wasn't until Matilda had begun to clear the table that Aunt Adelaide turned to Harleigh and said, "Now listen carefully, Harleigh. It has been decided that since you do not seem to be ready to be a trustworthy member of the Weatherby family, we will need to have a serious discussion

about enrolling you in an institution where you might learn to behave in a more responsible manner. Do you have anything to say?"

Harleigh met her steely glare steady-eyed, but all he said was, "No. Nothing that would make any difference."

"I see." Aunt Adelaide went on, "This morning I have an early appointment in town, so I'm afraid our discussion will have to be postponed until later. Perhaps this afternoon." To Uncle Edgar she said, "In the meantime, Harleigh will go back to his old study schedule." Turning back to Harleigh, she added, "So on Mondays and Wednesdays you will report to the library as usual at nine o'clock."

And that was that. Back in the Aerie, Harleigh gathered up his books and then sat down to wait until nine. There would be a robbery today while Aunt Adelaide was gone, or there wouldn't be, and there wasn't anything Harleigh could do about it. And if a lot of money that might have been used to keep Weatherby House from collapsing into ruins disappeared forever, that was how it would have to be. That was just how . . .

Suddenly Harleigh looked at his watch, picked up his books, and started downstairs. He did ask himself why, but he didn't try to answer the question. There was no answer, and he wasn't looking for one. There wasn't even an answer to "What?"—as in, "What do you think you're doing?"

But he kept on going until he reached the second floor, where he crossed the landing to a door that led out onto a small balcony. By peering from behind one of the balcony's decorative pillars, he had a good view of the driveway. He'd only waited a few minutes when he began to hear the noisy old Buick, and then watched it head for the main gate. But as he watched Aunt Adelaide leave for town, Harleigh couldn't help wondering if, somewhere behind another Weatherby House window, Junior was watching too.

Back now on the grand marble stairs that led down to the entry hall, Harleigh had a serious argument with himself about which direction he was going to go when he reached the main floor. Would he turn to the left toward the library and a slightly early lesson with Uncle Edgar, or to the right in the direction of the recital hall and . . . and what?

*I won't go far,* he told himself as he started down the wide dimly lit west corridor. *Just close enough to hear if he's tearing up the floorboards. That's sure to be noisy enough to be heard from that end of the drawing room. I'll just wait there for a few minutes, or maybe in the poolroom, and see if I hear anything. He won't see me. I'll be careful not to let him see me.*

That's what he told himself, but when he passed the drawing room door and then the one to the poolroom he didn't stop, and it wasn't until he had reached the recital hall when he began to hear it. Just what he had been expecting:

a series of sharp splintering thuds that came from the direction of the stage. Harleigh paused for only a second, and then, as if drawn by a magnet, he opened the door to Aunt Adelaide's recital hall bedroom and peered inside.

The heavy velvet curtains had been pulled aside, and on the stage a huge hulk of a man was at work. As Harleigh watched, Junior bent to lay aside a large ax and pick up an enormous crowbar, and then bent again to thrust it into the damaged floor. Harleigh didn't say anything, he was sure of that, but perhaps he gasped or even moaned, because suddenly Junior turned and stared directly at him.

As Harleigh was backing out into the hall, several things happened simultaneously. Junior pulled the crowbar out of the shattered planks and jumped down off the stage. And at the same time, a voice whispered, "Here. Come with me," and something tugged at Harleigh's sleeve. Dropping his books, Harleigh turned and followed a familiar shadowy shape that dashed down the hall through a door and into — total darkness.

Whispering, "Allegra. Where are you?" he staggered forward, only to fall over a large bulky object.

The voice was Allegra's, the dead, musky smell meant he was in the smoking room, and the object he'd fallen over was one of the fat, overstuffed chairs.

"Allegra?" Harleigh said. "It's so dark. Where are you?"

"Shh," she answered. "I closed all the blinds. Here. I'm over here."

Crawling in the direction of the voice, Harleigh found himself next to Allegra in the far corner of the room behind another one of the bulky, toad-shaped chairs.

"Where did you . . ." Harleigh was beginning to whisper when the smoking room door was flung open and a monstrous figure appeared in the opening. With his huge bulk blotting out what little light might have come in from the hall, Junior was staring into almost total darkness, and as his hulking shape moved forward there was a grunt, followed by a thudding crash, a howl, and a string of oaths. It seemed that Junior, too, had fallen over a chair.

On his feet again, Junior began to talk. "Come on out, kid," he said. "I know you're in here. You come out right now and I won't hurt you." His voice softened from a growl to a wheedling whine. "We'll just talk things over. Maybe make some kind of a deal. Okay?"

Behind the chair in the corner, Harleigh and Allegra lay low. Long seconds passed, and Junior muttered again and then apparently began to swing the crowbar, thudding it into chairs and against walls, tables, and finally the door to the poolroom. As the door disintegrated, Junior moved toward the light, opened what was left of the door, and disappeared into the poolroom.

"Now," Allegra whispered, "run." And they did, Allegra first and Harleigh close behind her. Out into the corridor, past the poolroom and into the solarium. They had almost reached the exterior doors that opened out onto the grassy field that had once been lawn, when they heard Junior's roar. "I see you, kid. Got you now. Here I come."

Harleigh ran fast, but out in the open, the length of Junior's legs gave him an advantage. By the time Allegra, with Harleigh close behind her, reached the first garden, Junior was very near. While jumping over crumbling stone walls and dodging around dead rose bushes and Roman statues, they maintained their slight lead, but the thunder of Junior's feet was again drawing closer when they reached the bamboo thicket.

The advantage was theirs then, as they slid through the well-known trails. Behind them they could hear swishing and slashing as Junior tried to keep up by forcing his way right through the heaviest stands of bamboo. When they reached the tree house clearing, they still could hear Junior's noisy progress, but he was not yet in sight.

It was then that Allegra slid to a stop, and turning back to Harleigh, she whispered, "Go that way. Go to the maze. I have to go over the fence." Putting her hands on his chest, she gave him a little shove and then turned away on the path

that led toward the fence and the tree where Harleigh had seen her fly.

Harleigh reached out to stop her, but his hand only closed on one of the long ragged tatters of her dress, and then she was gone, and on the other side of the clearing Junior burst out of the bamboo.

Harleigh ran toward the maze.

# Chapter Twenty-three

Once more Junior was close behind Harleigh as he reached the dead tree that blocked the entrance to the maze. Too close. If he'd been there only a few seconds sooner, he could have been safely hidden behind the branches of the dead tree by the time Junior burst out of the underbrush. But no such luck. Junior had arrived just in time to see Harleigh lift the branch that blocked the entrance, duck under it, and disappear. As he began to run down the path that he and Allegra had carved out of the surrounding hedge of yew, he heard Junior's triumphant roar. "Okay, you little rat. I got you now."

But he hadn't. Not yet. It was the yew itself that, for a time, gave Harleigh an advantage. The yew, and the fact that

neither Allegra nor Harleigh had been able to reach high enough to trim back the higher branches. Although the original passageway had been open to the sky, it was now only a narrow tunnel with a low overhang. So while Harleigh moved freely, Junior had to run bent almost double to keep the stiff branches from whacking his head and scratching his face. And then, as he began to get the hang of running in a crouching position, he apparently made another mistake. The kind of mistake that maze explorers had been making for centuries. With Harleigh momentarily out of his sight, Junior took the wrong turn.

When he realized that Junior was no longer right behind him, Harleigh stopped and looked back, trying to quickly figure out which wrong turn Junior had made. Was it one of the turnoffs that led to a dead end? Or perhaps one that curved around and circled back to rejoin the original passageway? There were several of both. It was important that he get it right, because the only way for him to escape was to get back to the entrance while Junior was wandering off toward a dead end. Harleigh could then leave the maze the way he'd come in. The only way he knew, since the only other exit was the one he and Allegra had almost, but not quite, found.

Harleigh had decided that Junior was out there some-where headed for a dead end, and he had begun to retrace

his steps, when a huge figure burst back onto the main corridor only a few yards away. Harleigh spun around and went
on running.

Once again Junior was close behind him. Close enough
so Harleigh could hear not only his thudding footsteps, but
also his wheezing breath. *Thud, thud, pant, pant,* and then an
angry yelp. Glancing back over his shoulder, Harleigh caught
a glimpse of a frantic scene, a wildly flailing Junior trying to
free his hair from a dangling branch of yew and in the
process dropping the heavy crowbar on his feet. And then,
with his hair finally free, he grabbed up the crowbar only to
find that he'd managed to hook its curved end around the
trunk of the nearest yew. He was still trying to jerk it free
when Harleigh reached the place where he and Allegra had
quit working only two days before. Where their progress
had stopped, leaving the original exit still unlocated. And
leaving Harleigh in a dead-end trap.

But just as he began to panic, Harleigh suddenly remembered what Allegra had said about being almost there.
Almost to the exit. And she had said it while she was lying
on the ground, reaching into a tiny tunnel that her shears
had started.

And then Harleigh was on his knees, and a moment later
flat on his stomach wriggling into the tunnel, and continuing to wriggle until first his hands and then his head, and

finally the rest of his body, were clear of the yew hedge, and he was able to jump to his feet.

He was free. Standing up, Harleigh looked around, recognizing a familiar spot. A path he had been on many times before, that led around the curving exterior wall of the maze. He turned to go but then went down on his knees to peer back into the rabbit-hole-size tunnel. And there, only a few feet away, Junior's squinty eyes peered back at him. Junior had somehow managed to force his big head and shoulders into the tunnel and was now imprisoned, it seemed, in a snug cocoon of yew branches. As Harleigh watched in stunned amazement, Junior thrashed and roared without making the least bit of forward progress.

And quite possibly, unable to go back either. But you never knew with someone as strong and fierce as Junior. Tired as he was, Harleigh didn't dawdle on his way back to Weatherby House and his very belated appointment with Uncle Edgar.

# Chapter Twenty-four

Of course Uncle Edgar didn't believe him at first. Harleigh couldn't help feeling impatient with him, because there was no time to waste if something was going to be done about Junior before he managed to untangle himself from his yew tree trap. But at the same time, Harleigh wasn't able to blame Uncle Edgar too much. He couldn't help being aware that if someone else had told him such a wild story, he probably wouldn't have believed it either.

But of course positive proof, of a sort, was easily available if Uncle Edgar would just accompany him to Aunt Adelaide's recital hall and see for himself. Harleigh knew, however, that it wouldn't be easy to get Uncle Edgar to visit

a place he often referred to as the Throne Room of Adelaide the Great and probably hadn't set foot in for years.

Harleigh guessed right. It was only after he'd suggested, asked, and finally demanded that he come see for himself, that Uncle Edgar levered himself out of his chair and began to lumber down the entry hall. They had turned off into the west corridor and had almost reached the recital hall's double doors when they suddenly became aware of a hair-raising sound. Aunt Adelaide's wheelchair.

They froze in horror, at first turning their eyes and then their heads, in time to see the wheelchair rounding the corner and hear Aunt Adelaide's scratchy voice demanding, "What's this? What is going on here?"

Harleigh stared at Uncle Edgar, hoping he would begin the explanation, but Uncle Edgar only stared back. At last Harleigh turned to face Aunt Adelaide's steely glare and began to stammer, "We—we were just going to—I was just going to show Uncle Edgar what Junior did to your room. To the floor of the stage, that is. See, what happened is . . . Well, Junior was just starting to chop a hole in the floor when . . ." His voice trailed off in despair. Waving one arm in the general direction of the recital hall, he finished weakly, "Come and see. I'll show you."

While Uncle Edgar held one of the doors open, they filed through: Harleigh first, right behind him the wheelchair

pushed by Cousin Josephine, and last of all Uncle Edgar.

And there it was. All of it, in plain view. The stage curtains were still pulled open and the recital hall's bright lights
were spilling in to reveal the stage floor, where Junior's huge
ax was lying beside a gaping, roughly cut hole.

They moved closer, rounded the rosewood desk and
the enormous canopied bed, and continued on to the very
edge of the stage. And then Aunt Adelaide was pointing
at Harleigh and screeching, "You. You ungrateful, destruc-
tive, incorrigible . . ." Her voice had trailed off into an
unintelligible screech when it happened. Suddenly lurching
to one side, Aunt Adelaide collapsed limply over one arm
of the chair.

Harleigh and Uncle Edgar stared at Aunt Adelaide and
then at Cousin Josephine, who was calmly turning the chair
while she steadied Aunt Adelaide with one hand. "Here,"
she said to Uncle Edgar, "help me get her onto the bed.
She'll be all right soon."

"You mean she's not—not dying, or anything?"
Harleigh gasped.

Josephine shook her head. "No," she said. "Not likely.
She's been like this before. It happens when she gets too
excited. She'll probably sleep for a while, and when she wakes
up she'll be as good as . . ." Josephine paused and then, smiling grimly, went on, "That is, she'll be the same as always."

So it wasn't until Aunt Adelaide had been lifted onto her bed, her shoes removed and her pillow fluffed, that the rest of them turned back to the damaged stage.

"There," Harleigh said. "See, I heard this loud chopping noise and I came in to see what was happening. And there Junior was . . . There he was chopping this hole, and when he saw me, he started chasing me with a crowbar and I—well, I . . ." He trailed off and turned to Uncle Edgar. "And like I told you, he's stuck in the maze now, or at least he was. That's what I've been trying to tell you."

There followed quite a pause while the three of them looked at each other and then, uncertainly, back at the hole in the stage floor, until Harleigh began to realize it was going to be up to him to do something.

"All right," he said. "Come on. Let's find out what's in there."

The first step was to get Uncle Edgar up onto the stage, which was only accomplished with a lot of pushing and pulling. And then came the problem of getting him back on his feet, which he finally managed himself by scooting to the upright piano and using it to balance on as he straightened up. At last Uncle Edgar was on his feet and dusted off a little, and Harleigh was free to peer down the hole. But the light was bad and the hole was small. Nothing was visible.

While Cousin Josephine went to get a flashlight, it

occurred to Harleigh that there must be another way. Somehow it just didn't seem likely that a first-generation Weatherby, or even a second-generation direct descendant, would store something valuable in a place you could only get to by chopping up valuable hardwood flooring. Somehow it seemed more likely . . .

Moving around the stage, he checked out the three steps that led down to the stage door, but they seemed to be firmly and immovably built in. And on the stage itself there were only the two ancient pianos, the three-legged grand and the bulky, old-fashioned upright that sat back against the far wall. Looking around, Harleigh studied the scene and began to wonder—why two pianos? And then he asked Uncle Edgar to help him try to move the big old upright.

And so they did, but it wasn't easy. Even with Uncle Edgar's weight leaning against it, the piano moved to one side only very slowly. But move it did, leaving exposed a large, dusty rectangle, which it had covered for many, many years. And in the middle of that rectangle, a well-constructed trapdoor.

The trapdoor lifted easily and they all peered down, saying things like, "My God, would you look at that!" That was Uncle Edgar.

Cousin Josephine said, "Stand aside. I'll do it," followed

by, "Oh my goodness. I can't go down there. There are sure to be spiders."

So it was Harleigh who was sent down to explore. Carrying the flashlight Josephine had provided, he went down two steep steps to where a collection of metal boxes sat in neat rows, covered by many years of ancient dust. And it was also Harleigh who, one by one, dragged the boxes to the steps and lifted them up to Josephine and Uncle Edgar.

Most of the boxes were not very heavy, but a few others were, and they rattled in a muffled but vaguely metallic way—an exciting, possibly golden, sound. But all of them were firmly locked with small rusty padlocks. It wasn't until all eleven of them had been brought up onto the stage that Harleigh caught his breath—and remembered about Junior.

# Chapter Twenty-five

By the time Uncle Edgar called the police, almost two hours had passed since Harleigh had left Junior Weatherby stuck in the maze's overgrown exit. But at last three Riverbend officers drove up the circular drive, pulled up to the front entrance of Weatherby House, and were ushered into the entrance hall by Uncle Edgar, where they stood around looking confused and amazed while Harleigh and Uncle Edgar and Cousin Josephine kept interrupting each other as they tried to explain what had happened and who had done it.

Harleigh was frustrated by how long it took for the officers to begin to show as much interest in Junior's crimes as they did in their surroundings. Obviously they had never

been in Weatherby House before, or anything quite like it.

"It seems he located the long-lost Weatherby treasure," Uncle Edgar was saying. "With a metal detector."

"In Adelaide Weatherby's bedroom," Cousin Josephine broke in. "Under the stage."

The policeman who was taking notes paused with his pen in the air. "Under the what?" he asked.

"Under the *stage*," Cousin Josephine repeated, sounding impatient, almost rude, as if it was perfectly normal to have a stage in your bedroom.

Uncle Edgar was still trying to explain why they didn't exactly know what it was that had almost been stolen, when Harleigh interrupted him by saying, "And when I saw what he was doing, he tried to kill me with a crowbar." It wasn't until then that the officers began to pay more attention.

"And this person who attacked you with a crowbar, you're saying you recognized this person." The policeman named Sergeant Marino seemed quite interested now.

"Of course I did," Harleigh said. "He lives here. His name is Junior Weatherby."

"Oh, I see. Junior?" The note-taking officer was smiling condescendingly at Harleigh. "And is Junior as big as you are?"

That made Harleigh mad. "He's big," he said through clenched teeth. "A lot bigger than you are."

"Is this true?" Sergeant Marino asked Uncle Edgar. "A grown man tried to attack this boy with a crowbar?" After Uncle Edgar said it was true, the police got down to business and agreed to inspect the scene of the crime.

Then came a rather slow procession down the west corridor: Harleigh, Uncle Edgar, Cousin Josephine, and the three bug-eyed police officers. And on into the recital hall, where Aunt Adelaide was still sleeping soundly and snoring loudly in her canopied bed. And then, finally, they were all up on the stage, where the large ax still lay next to the gaping hole in the hardwood floor. And where eleven dusty and rusty boxes were now neatly stacked next to the upright piano.

Then there was another long delay while Uncle Edgar explained to the police officers how it was that no one yet knew what was in the boxes, and how whatever it was belonged to Harleigh and his father as the direct descendants of the Weatherby estate.

All of it, all the explanations, inspections, and careful questioning, had taken an endless amount of time and, just as Harleigh feared, by the time he and the three officers finally reached the spot where he had last seen Junior trapped in the tiny prickly tunnel, he was no longer there. All the officers took turns getting down on their knees and staring into the hole, and by the time they had finished they were once again asking the kind of questions that made it

clear that they didn't believe a word of what Harleigh had been telling them. Questions like, "And when you last saw this very large man, he was crawling through that little hole?"

It was, Harleigh had to admit, a little hard to believe. He offered to take the police to the maze entrance, and through to where the tunnel started, but they didn't seem interested.

"How long would that take?" Sergeant Marino asked.

"Only about half an hour if you know the way," Harleigh said. "I could show you."

Sergeant Marino looked at his watch and shook his head. "Maybe some other day," he said. "Right now we need to get back on duty."

As the three police officers, and a frustrated and embarrassed Harleigh, were on their way back through the overgrown jungle that had once been the famous Weatherby gardens, they began to hear a crackling, crashing sound that seemed to be coming from the bamboo thicket. As they stopped and turned to look back, a huge man burst into view only a few yards away. No longer carrying his crowbar, his face and arms covered in bloody scrapes and scratches, and his clothing in tatters, an almost unrecognizable Junior was waving his arms in the air and babbling wildly. His eyes were wide and staring, but when he saw Harleigh he froze, and then staggered forward, yelling, "There you are, you little rat. Now I'll get you."

Scared, but at the same time relieved to have this sudden proof of his story, Harleigh ducked behind the police officers, who soon had Junior handcuffed and under control.

As the police escorted him off to their car, Harleigh, trailing behind at a safe distance, heard Junior saying he'd been trapped in what he called "those ghost bushes" for hours. "For days," he raved. "For years, maybe. See, those things keep changing. They don't stay still. Just when you get it figured out, they change." Lowering his voice, he almost whispered, "And there are voices in those bushes. Voices that tell you which way to go to get out, but they lie. They always lie."

At one point he stopped to look back at Harleigh and then went on babbling. "He'll lie too. He'll say I was going to kill him. But that's a lie. Those bushes wouldn't let me catch him."

Harleigh followed as far as the gate and watched from a distance as the police carefully loaded the still ranting and raving Junior into their patrol car, before he returned to Weatherby House.

Not only Uncle Edgar, but also Cousins Josephine and Alden were waiting for Harleigh in the library. They listened in fascinated silence as Harleigh told about the capture and how Junior thought the yew trees had been talking to him and telling him lies. He finished his story by saying, "It sounded to me like he really cracked up."

Cousin Alden said that he wasn't surprised. "Not surprised at all," he said. "Since the day I first met him I've always felt that particular would-be Weatherby had a few bats in his belfry."

After they'd finished discussing what might happen to Junior and whether it would be jail or an institution, Harleigh asked Cousin Josephine about Aunt Adelaide.

"It's so strange," Cousin Josephine said. "She woke up and let me help her into her wheelchair, but she hasn't said anything. Not a word. When I asked her if she wanted to go to lunch, she shook her head, so I brought her a sandwich and she ate most of it with none of her usual complaints. And when I asked if I should call her doctor, she only shook her head again. But she still hasn't said anything. Not a word."

"Amazing," Uncle Edgar said. "Really amazing."

Harleigh knew what he meant. A speechless Aunt Adelaide was not an easy thing to picture.

Harleigh was still trying to imagine it when Cousin Alden asked when they were going to open the boxes. Cousin Josephine looked over to where the eleven metal boxes were now stacked on one of the library tables. "Soon, I guess," she said. "But it looks like a big job. Maybe we should wait until after lunch."

Uncle Edgar pulled out his pocket watch and exclaimed in surprise.

"Well, would you look at that," he said. "Don't know when I've let a mealtime sneak up on me like that. But I do think you're right. Those boxes have been waiting a long time. I don't think one more hour will make any difference. Come on, all of you. Let's not keep Matilda waiting any longer."

When Harleigh and Uncle Edgar reached the kitchen, there was another difference. Cousin Alden, who as a non-Weatherby had never before been permitted to eat in the kitchen, came right in and sat down by his wife.

Harleigh was hungrier than usual, and when he took a second helping Matilda smiled encouragingly. He smiled back and said, "Good stuff."

While they were all eating, Cousin Alden brought up the subject of the boxes. What he wanted to know was whether anyone had any objection to letting him watch the opening of the boxes. "I would have known better than to even think of asking if Aunt Adelaide was still in charge," he told them, "since I'm only a Weatherby by marriage. But under the present circumstances . . ." He grinned at Harleigh and Uncle Edgar. "Okay?" he asked. "If I promise not to steal anything? Not even some ideas for my next novel?"

So Harleigh gave him permission, and then, because she'd obviously heard the whole discussion and must be curious, he asked Matilda if she'd like to come too.

Everyone seemed surprised, particularly Matilda. But when Harleigh asked her again, she grinned and nodded, took off her apron, and followed the procession to the library—and the opening of the boxes.

It took a long time even after Uncle Edgar produced a bolt cutter that was able to cut through the rusty padlocks. Several of the boxes were full of different kinds of certificates printed in fancy, old-fashioned lettering—things that Uncle Edgar said might, or might not, be very valuable. But then came a more interesting find. One of the heaviest boxes was packed with leather sacks full of coins. Some of the coins seemed to be of nickel and silver, but some others were obviously solid gold. That really caused some excitement.

After that were a couple of boxes that held stacks of paper money. American paper money, dated in the late eighteen hundreds and the early nineteen hundreds, and looking like nothing Harleigh had ever seen before.

Before the last box was opened, several hours had gone by. Matilda, who had seemed very interested for a while, excused herself and left to start dinner. She wasn't the only one. Harleigh, too, found himself losing interest now and then. Especially after he happened to rub his head, and the sore spot reminded him of another important question. The one concerning whether he really was growing—or not. So

he left the box-opening operation briefly while he went to measure himself under the portrait of Harleigh the First.

Sure enough, he could no longer stand below the picture in the spot where he use to measure himself to see how much he would have to grow to reach the frame of Harleigh the First's portrait. Back then there had always been an inch or two to spare, but now the sharp gilded edge of the frame was exactly level with his sore spot. The sore spot that was *halfway up the back of his head.* He was grinning as he went back to join the group.

There were also a couple of other times when the discoveries were a bit of a letdown, and Harleigh, who'd had a rough day and not much sleep the night before, came close to dozing off. For instance, one whole box was packed full of letters that seemed to be either to or from lawyers — Harleigh the First's lawyers as well as a bunch from lawyers for other people.

But at last the final box was opened and inspected and everyone got up to go. "So," Harleigh asked Uncle Edgar. "Are we rich? Will it be enough to . . ."

"To what? What did you have in mind?"

Harleigh thought of mentioning the tumbled turrets, the cracked windows, or even the ancient bathrooms, but he found he was just too tired to give it any serious thought.

Mumbling something, he headed for the kitchen and a meal he was almost too tired to eat.

It wasn't until he was getting ready for bed that night that he put his hand into his pants pocket and felt something soft and filmy tangle around his fingers. Puzzled, he pulled it out and smoothed it flat on his knee before he realized it was the piece of Allegra's dress that had torn off when he was trying to keep her from running away to the place where she—but not Harleigh—could fly over the wall. There wasn't much to it. He sat there on the edge of his bed for a while looking at the soft, almost sheer, scrap of pale, silvery material and wondering. Wondering, first of all, how she happened to be in Weatherby House when Junior started chasing him. Did that mean she'd found a way to get back into the house whenever she wanted to? And if so, how and where?

She'd said something about doors that were unlocked. And something else about doors that were locked now that didn't use to be. Like maybe the door to his room in the Aerie?

Remembering the times he'd thought he'd heard someone on the stairs and even trying the latch on his door, Harleigh went on wondering, but not for very long. It had been a long, hard day.

# Chapter Twenty-six

The next few days were busy and interesting most of the time, and even when they weren't particularly busy, they were certainly different. One of the biggest changes was because of Aunt Adelaide. Her silence alone took some getting used to. After a day or two she did start coming to meals in the kitchen again, at least part of the time, but the fact that she didn't have anything to say about Cousin Alden being there too, eating Matilda's cooking, was a large difference all by itself.

According to Cousin Josephine, Aunt Adelaide continued to shake her head when she was asked if she wanted to see her doctor, but when she still wasn't talking on the third day, Cousin Josephine called him anyway. So the doctor came,

and afterward Cousin Josephine said he seemed to be baffled too, but he thought it might have been a stroke.

"A stroke of luck," Cousin Alden said, which Cousin Josephine said was heartless. However, she didn't argue when he suggested that since Aunt Adelaide obviously wasn't going to object, maybe they could all stop with the ridiculous family titles now. So they stopped the Aunt, Uncle, Cousin business, which everybody agreed was a relief.

The one title that stuck, at least partially, was Aunt Adelaide's. Somehow no one seemed to be able to manage just plain Adelaide, so it became simply Aunt. But at least it should be Aunt with a capital A, Josephine said, and her husband said he thought he could go that far. "So the next time you hear me saying Aunt," he told Harleigh, "be sure you listen for the capital A."

But it didn't seem to Harleigh that Aunt was unhappy. She still came to the kitchen for most of her meals, but if some of the recent changes—like the people who now ate there—made her angry, it didn't show.

There was another big change in Aunt's life, and that was TV. In the past Aunt Adelaide had never allowed a television set anywhere near Weatherby House. But then Josephine, with Ralph's help, installed one in the recital hall, and Aunt soon became addicted. Josephine sometimes worried that watching that much TV was abnormal,

but Alden said he thought a quietly watching Aunt seemed a lot less abnormal than the previous one had ever been.

There were other changes too, most of which grew out of the existence of the treasure. It did turn out to be worth a lot of money, or would be eventually, when Edgar finished sorting it out. Of course the gold coins were very valuable, and some of the certificates and deeds with the fancy printing could be converted into cash, but it was a long, involved process. A lot of the paper money was too old to be worth much except to people who collected such things, but it would take a while to find the right buyers.

When Edgar began to complain that he was swamped by all the paperwork, Harleigh remembered that Sheila had been a secretary and suggested that maybe she could help. When he asked her, she seemed delighted. So much so that her eyebrows tilted at an entirely new angle and pretty much stayed that way, which gave her a more agreeable appearance. She did turn out to be good at all the things secretaries are supposed to do. And being so busy with typing and phoning and mailing left less time for weeping and wailing, which made her a lot more popular with her neighbors in the west wing.

There were other people who started being involved in sorting out the treasure. People such as A. J., who still

hadn't passed his bar exam after more than twenty years of trying, but who nevertheless knew quite a bit about the law and was able to help keep everything legal.

But in spite of how much it helped to have a secretary and a lawyer, Edgar was still terribly busy, and Harleigh's lessons began to be a lot shorter, if they happened at all. And when they did happen, they tended to be mostly discussions instead of planned study sessions. Harleigh didn't mind, really, especially when the subjects discussed turned out to be things that mattered to him. Like the day that they talked all morning about Harleigh's famous ancestor, Harleigh J. Weatherby the First.

It was a subject they'd covered many times before and never agreed on. It had always seemed to Harleigh that it was all very well to criticize someone if you were just as rich and famous as they were—or in this case, had been. But when poor, old, lazy, overweight Edgar did it . . . well, there *was* such a thing as sour grapes. But then Edgar showed Harleigh the box full of letters from lawyers.

Of course Harleigh didn't read all of them, but Edgar said the ones he'd picked out were pretty representative. Some of the letters to Harleigh the First's lawyers were from other lawyers who were working for people who had been kicked off their property because Harleigh J. Weatherby decided he wanted it. Several of the victims were other

businessmen, but there were also quite a few letters from people like widows and orphans.

One of the letters that Edgar seemed especially eager for Harleigh to read said:

Dear Mr. Weatherby,

As the minister of the Riverbend First Presbyterian Church where Mrs. McIntyre and her family are members, I am writing to inform you that due to the death of Mrs. McIntyre's husband and her own serious illness, she will not be able to pay her December rent on time. She has asked me to petition you to allow her to put off payment for the time being. Her two oldest children have quit school and have found work in the Weatherby Garment Factory, and she is hoping that their earnings will make it possible for her to repay her debts in the near future.

—Rev G. H. Smithson

The answering letter was from one of Harleigh the First's lawyers, and all it said was: "Please inform Mrs. McIntyre that her request is denied. She will be given two weeks to vacate the premises."

And then there were the letters from H. J. Weatherby's lawyers. Those were the really nasty ones full of threats

about what the Weatherby company would do to people who didn't just shut up and get out of Mr. Weatherby's way. By the time Harleigh Four had finished reading, he found that when he looked up at the portrait of his famous ancestor, it was from a slightly different point of view.

Just a day or two after Harleigh Four read the lawyers' letters, his father showed up, as unexpectedly and unannounced as usual. The news about the treasure and the situation with Aunt Adelaide had finally reached him in Australia, and he had, he said, headed for home immediately, stopping off only once to examine an unusual building in San Francisco. And then there he was, in the midst of all the changes.

At first Edgar had to spend a lot of time filling him in on all the money the Weatherby family now had, and for a while he seemed to be paying close attention. For a few days he even got involved in choosing a contractor to repair the fallen turrets, and in drawing up some plans for the new bathrooms. But a few days later he lost interest and took off on a trip to study the Taj Mahal.

The first Monday morning after the Wednesday that changed everything, Harleigh went back to the tree house. Allegra wasn't there, but she had been there recently, either on Saturday or Sunday. Harleigh knew her visit had been recent because there had been rain on Friday, and the note

he found in the cracked teacup was not smudged or damp. The note said:

Dear Harleigh,

    I have to go away now. I'll come back someday, but I don't know when.

    —Allegra

Harleigh took the note home and put it away in a special hiding place at the back of one of the Aerie's cabinets, where he kept the scrap of her tattered dress. The next few weeks were a busy and exciting time for Harleigh Four. But no matter how busy he was with all the things that were happening at Weatherby House, he went back to the black walnut tree every Monday and Wednesday morning and waited for at least an hour. But Allegra never came.

# Chapter Twenty-seven

And then it was September, and with it came cooler weather and some serious discussions about what was going to be done about Harleigh Four's education. The thing was, it just wasn't happening anymore with Edgar. He and Harleigh did have some lengthy sessions now and then, but they were mostly spent deciding things about the House and the money.

Harleigh could see that it would be too much to expect Edgar to go back to being his tutor and still go on investing, controlling, and arranging to spend all that money. It would be too much work even for someone a lot younger and more energetic than Edgar.

"So what *are* we going to do?" he asked Harleigh. "It

looks like it won't be too long before you are going to have to take over being responsible for not only all the Weatherby assets, but also the lives of quite a few direct, and not so direct, Weatherby descendants. And to handle all that you're going to need to know your way around this complicated world."

Harleigh more or less agreed—at least he had begun to, rather recently. He also realized that only a few weeks ago he might not have agreed at all. In thinking back over the recent past, he remembered feeling that he already knew just about everything he needed to know, along with exactly where he wanted to go with his life. But somehow, he didn't know exactly how or why, he was now a little less sure of—of what? Of what he ought to do about a lot of the people who lived in Weatherby House, for one thing, along with what he might want to do with all the money that old Harleigh the First had squeezed out of all sorts of people and then stashed away under the stage in his grand recital hall.

At any rate, for whatever reason, and partly against his will, he found himself thinking that he still had a lot to learn. But where? That was the big question.

One thing he was sure of was that he didn't want to be sent to the Hardacre Military Academy that Aunt had been so crazy about. And it seemed that the only other

choice would be to go back to the Riverbend schools; at this point probably to seventh or eighth grade at the junior high. At least that was what Edgar seemed to think. When Edgar brought up that possibility, Harleigh nodded reluctantly and sighed.

"As bad as all that? Here. Tell me about it." Edgar patted the chair next to his. They were in the library at the time, where they had just finished going over stacks of letters and notebooks that kept track of what was being done with the money. So Harleigh sat down again and told him.

"Well, some of them, boys mostly, but a few girls, too, thought it was really funny that I was so—so short. And then someone started calling me Hardly instead of Harleigh. They'd even call me Hardly in front of the teachers, and then they'd just pretend that they had mispronounced my name by accident. And besides that—"

Edgar patted his shoulder and said he got the picture. "But things are quite different now," he said. "For one thing, you're bigger now. You know you really have been growing lately, don't you?"

Harleigh nodded. He knew now that it was true. Ever since the day he'd cracked his head on the picture frame, he'd been measuring himself at least once a day, and there was no doubt about it. He really was growing, and fast. "But I'm still not as big as a lot of them are," he said.

"True." Edgar nodded. "But physically you're probably already as big as some of them, and in a lot of other areas you're definitely on your way toward being at the top of the heap. Take my word for it, Harleigh. You're growing in more ways than one."

But when Harleigh still didn't seem too pleased with the idea of returning to Riverbend, Edgar had some more advice to offer. "Believe me, Harleigh," he said. "I understand the problem. Remember, I was one of the 'lucky' boys who got sent off to Hardacre as a teenager. A slightly rebellious, and already more than slightly chubby, teenager." He shrugged and curved his wide lips into a sour smile before he went on. "I spent a couple of pretty miserable months. But then I discovered a trick that helped a lot."

"Oh, yeah?" Harleigh asked. "So what trick was that?"

"The trick was—to make all the other boys believe that I didn't care. That I didn't care what any of them did or said. It didn't happen immediately, and at first I definitely was putting on an act. But after I'd worked at it for a while, I found out that it really was true. As soon as I really didn't care what they did, they stopped doing it. Kind of spoiled the fun, I guess."

At the time Harleigh enjoyed Edgar's story about his "trick," but he didn't take it too seriously. However, when

the semester started there they were again—all the same old teasers and tormentors who remembered him from fifth grade and hadn't forgotten how much fun they'd had calling him Hardly and some other insulting names. But after a while he began to see some changes.

For one thing, a new and different problem had cropped up at Weatherby House. One that Harleigh had to help solve. Actually, he'd learned about it a couple of weeks before school started when the Farleys, two of the elderly descendants who lived in the west wing, came to talk to Harleigh and Edgar about their grandson.

It seemed this grandson, whose name was Tyler, was about to become homeless. That is, his mother, who was a single parent, was going to have to be in the hospital for a long time, and there wasn't any place for Tyler to live. Unless it could be with his Weatherby grandparents.

"Of course," John Farley, the elderly husband, said, "we would never have even considered asking Aunt Adelaide if Tyler could come to stay with us. We knew how strict her rules were about allowing any children on the premises." The old man paused to glance at Harleigh and then went on, "At least children who weren't direct descendants. But recently we've begun to wonder if . . ."

Edgar looked at Harleigh for a long, thoughtful moment before he said, "What do you think, Harleigh? We need a

decision here, and I guess it's up to you to make it. Any ideas?"

Afterward Harleigh wasn't entirely sure who came up with the solution, but he knew he'd had a hand in it. The solution was that people who were going to be closest to a problem ought to be involved in deciding what to do about it.

So there was a conference in the library attended by all the west wing people, which included Matilda and Sheila and the Galworthy sisters and several others. And after John and Sally Farley finished telling their grandson's sad story, Sheila and both of the Galworthys were sobbing and even Matilda seemed about to, and the verdict was that they'd all be happy to have Tyler as a neighbor.

Tyler arrived two weeks after the school year had already started at Riverbend Junior High, and it turned out that he, too, was in the eighth grade. But when Harleigh met his new classmate and fellow Weatherby House resident, his immediate reaction was a stunned, *Great! Just what I need.*

That meeting happened in Weatherby House's grand entry hall, and having seen lots of other people's reaction to its size and splendor, Harleigh wasn't surprised by Tyler's open-mouthed amazement. However, in Tyler's case that open mouth did make his extremely buck teeth a little more noticeable. Those teeth, along with the fact that he was incredibly skinny and had hair that looked like it had been combed by an eggbeater, made for a really bad first impression. Harleigh's first impression was that having to take Tyler with him to Riverbend Junior High wasn't going to make his own life any easier.

And it certainly didn't, except briefly, while most of the really dedicated torturers were too busy going after poor old toothy Tyler to torment Harleigh as much as usual. But that didn't last very long, because for some strange reason Tyler didn't seem to mind. When Frankie Nelson and his gang of really smart-mouthed guys went after Tyler, he just grinned as if he thought it was all in good fun and went right on with whatever he was doing. His reaction didn't make any sense to Harleigh until it suddenly occurred to him that maybe he was doing what Edgar said he'd done — pretending he didn't care. But when he asked Tyler about it he said no, that wasn't it. He wasn't pretending.

"I guess I'm just used to it," he said. "It was a lot worse where I was before I came here. It's great living in Weatherby House with my grandparents, and . . ." He grinned at Harleigh. "And having somebody to go to school with is . . ." He shrugged, and his grin was even toothier than usual. "That part is really — okay."

And Harleigh managed to hold his tongue, but what he was thinking was a sarcastic, *Well, I'm glad somebody's happy.*

# Chapter Twenty-eight

As September turned into October and then moved on into November, some things at Riverbend Junior High began to improve, at least for Tyler. One of the big improvements was that after three months of eating Matilda's cooking, he wasn't nearly so skinny, and the Galworthy sister who had once worked in a beauty shop had managed to tame his hair down a little bit. And then one day, after another conference with Harleigh, Edgar announced that he'd decided that having braces put on Tyler's teeth would be a worthwhile investment of a bit of the Weatherby treasure.

The braces made a big difference, and more quickly than you might think. Even before the slant of Tyler's teeth had

changed all that much, there was a noticeable change in his social life. It just so happened that several of the most popular kids in the class had braces that year, so it seemed that Tyler suddenly became part of an exclusive in-group. An in-group that gradually, because Tyler insisted on it, began to include Harleigh as well.

At home Harleigh went on visiting the tree house when he had a little free time, which wasn't all that often anymore. He would climb up, easily now, and think about how much things had changed since he had first been there. He thought about Allegra, too, and wondered where she was and if she was ever going to come back.

But then one day, when he happened to have a little extra time, he found his way back to the tall tree where he had watched while Allegra had somehow managed to jump—or swing, or fly—over the fence. Studying the impossibly difficult climb to reach the top branches, and then even farther up, the open space that she must have somehow crossed to get to the other side, he began to feel that the whole Allegra thing must have been a kind of fantasy. Of course she really had existed. He had the piece of her dress and her good-bye note to prove it. So parts of the Allegra story had actually happened, but other parts must have been mostly his imagination. She really must have been, not really a fantasy, perhaps, but something pretty close to it.

Meanwhile, back at Weatherby House Aunt was still watching television, so Harleigh and Edgar had to go on making a lot of important decisions—such as whether there was enough money now to hire gardeners. And they did. Not the huge crews that had once worked on the Weatherby property, but a couple of hard-working guys who gradually began to replant lawns and flower beds, and get the water flowing again in the Italian garden's fountain.

And then one Saturday in November, Harleigh decided to show Tyler, as well as Tom and Pete, the two new gardeners, the entrance to the maze. It took a whole afternoon, and all three of them were what Tyler called "absolutely *a-mazed!*"

Tom and Pete immediately set to work finishing the job that Harleigh and Allegra had started, and before long most of the Weatherby House residents, except for a few of the most ancient ones, had visited the maze and been "a-mazed" at its size and beauty and the incredibly complicated route that finally led to the exit. But only on Saturdays, when Harleigh and Tyler could be available to rescue them after an hour or so and show them how to find their way out.

Dinners were another thing that changed that winter. Starting in December, nearly all of the Weatherby descendants, maybe fourteen or fifteen people at a time, began to meet, now and then, in the big dining hall for one of

Matilda's banquets. Only now Matilda had a lot of helpers, Weatherby descendants who might not be able to cook as well as she did, but who could peel and chop and stir, and help clean up the mess afterward.

At first Harleigh always sat next to Tyler at the banquets, but then Edgar suggested that the two of them should move around and sit with different people. "Why?" Harleigh wanted to know. "Tyler and I have things to talk about."

"I'm sure you do. But so do some of the rest of us. Why don't you give it a try?"

So Harleigh sighed and said he would, but when he told Tyler about it, he added that he thought it would be a bore listening to all the "olden days" stories. And sometimes it was. Some of the stories had parts that were boring or sad, or even both at once, but after a while he and Tyler agreed that if you kept on listening, a lot of the descendants' stories had some fairly interesting parts about things they'd lived through. Things like earthquakes or shipwrecks, or even attacks by poisonous snakes.

Later, on his way to the tower, Harleigh sometimes thought about stories and what Allegra had said about them. About how the walls of old houses were full of whispers and how, if you held your breath and listened closely, you could almost hear them. He had tried it. He'd stopped to listen, sometimes in one room and sometimes in another, without

a great deal of success. But if he didn't learn much from the walls that winter, he discovered that the real people who were living in Weatherby House did have interesting stories to tell, when they could get anyone to listen.

Quite often, when it was his turn to tell a story, Harleigh told about how Junior had tried to kill him with a crowbar and steal the Weatherby House treasure. That one always went over big with the descendants, no matter how many times they'd heard it before. Harleigh always tried to make it more exciting by mentioning some new and especially exciting details, such as how Junior had grabbed his foot as he started through the tunnel, and he'd had to kick his way free.

But one detail he never mentioned was Allegra. The part about Allegra, he'd decided, was just too fantastic, and the rest of the story, the part about Junior and the Weatherby treasure, definitely hadn't been a fantasy.

It was on a cold, drizzly Saturday morning that same winter that Harleigh discovered something that might possibly add a whole new chapter to the Allegra story. He happened to be looking through Edgar's copy of the *Riverbend Press*, something he didn't do all that often, when he noticed two pictures in a special section called "Riverbend Residents." The larger picture was of an old woman who had been, the story said, a resident of Riverbend for many years. But it

was a smaller photograph that suddenly grabbed Harleigh's attention. There were five people in that one, and under it was a caption that said, "The Famous Flying Fairchilds."

The story that went with the pictures said the old woman was Anna Fairchild, and she was the mother of Archibald Fairchild, who was in the second picture along with his wife and three daughters. Harleigh glanced at the picture of Archibald's family, looked back, and then stared for a long time. All five Fairchilds seemed to be wearing sleek, shiny costumes. Two of the daughters seemed to be almost full grown, but the smallest of the three, a very slender little girl, looked—looked strangely familiar. The Flying Fairchilds, the newspaper story said, were a family of acrobats and trapeze artists who had performed in many countries, all over the world.

Harleigh cut out the story and the two pictures and took them up to his room, where he spread them out on his bed next to the ragged scrap of Allegra's costume and the note he'd found in the teacup.

Sitting there on his bed, he moved the piece of cloth and the note and the pictures, arranging them in a special way. The piece of cloth first, because he got it first, and then the note, and finally the newspaper clippings. It was beginning to make a kind of pattern. A pattern, but with some important missing pieces.

The weather was a little better by the time Harleigh set out for the tree house that afternoon. Still gray and gloomy but no rain and very little wind. In the Italian garden the dolphin fountain was spouting again, and the marble gods and goddesses were sleek and white. But the weed-grown clearing that surrounded the tall black walnut tree looked the same as ever.

In the tree house everything—the rug, the walls, and the canvas roof—was slightly damp. Harleigh sat on the damp rug, looking at the broken teacup and the dead flowers in the tin can, and thinking over some of the things Allegra had told him about herself, and some other things she hadn't mentioned. Things that he now was beginning to be able to imagine.

It was easy to guess what her life had been like in Riverbend, living with her grandmother and probably hating it that she couldn't be with the rest of her famous family. After all the places she'd been and the exciting things she'd done, Riverbend must have seemed pretty dull—at least until she found Weatherby House.

So she'd discovered how to get over the fence, which would have been impossible for anyone who hadn't been trained to climb and "fly" across big, open spaces. Then, of course, because she was that sort of person, she'd started exploring everywhere. So she'd found things like the tree

house and the maze and Weatherby House. And because she was so crazy about old houses she started looking for a way to get inside. Then she'd found Harleigh, or he had found her, right there in the tree house clearing, and he turned out to be just what she was looking for — a way to get into Weatherby House.

The whole Allegra thing was — well, more than just a story because he himself had been a part of it, but there seemed to be some chapters that he hadn't known anything about and that he was just now beginning to understand.

Harleigh grinned, wondering if even a tree house's stained and splintery walls could whisper, if you knew how to listen. Reaching into his pocket, he took out the newspaper clippings and the ragged piece of cloth, and finally the note she'd left in the teacup, and spread them out on the braided rug. The small girl in the photo was certainly Allegra. The ragged bit of material looked as if it could have come from a costume very much like the one she was wearing in the picture.

And then came the note. The note that said she would be back someday. Harleigh thought that was probably true, and if it were, there would be new chapters to the Allegra story. In the meantime, all he could do was to try to listen.